THE HIGHLANDER'S LADY KNIGHT

MADELINE MARTIN

Sutherland, Scotland
May 1193

In the year since Cormac Sutherland had become Chieftain of the Sutherland clan, the crops had failed, the weather had turned foul, and his people were dying.

He swept his palm over his jaw and let his hand come to rest against the back of his neck where the muscles were knotted like a sailor's rope. His da had faced trials to be sure, but not in his first year as chieftain. And not like this.

He stared out the open window at the fields of tender shoots, all buried in an inch of water. The rain continued to fall at a steady rate, guaranteeing that the perpetual flood of water would not be absorbed and would wash out yet another crop. Also guaranteeing that the fragile new plants would likely die. Again.

As if the blight on the prior year's plants during harvest had not already devastated the clan.

"We could go back to the Rosses."

Cormac turned to face his twin, Graham. They both had dark, shoulder-length hair, bright green eyes and a height that bespoke of their strong lineage. Graham sat on the corner of Cormac's oversized desk with his arse settled on a stack of parchment.

"We canna go back to the Rosses." Cormac wrapped his hand at the back of his neck. "They already gave their excess grain stores to the MacDonalds. I sent a spy out to see how their crops are faring with the constant rain we've had. I expect him back shortly."

Graham shook his head and growled his aggravation. "The Rosses know we canna abide the MacDonalds."

"The Rosses are the only clan I know who had surplus crops in the last year." Cormac sighed and dropped his arm back to his side. "We either need more grain or more coin to have it carted in from farther away."

A knock sounded at the solar door, and Cormac bid them enter. A wiry young man with messy golden blond hair entered—Hamish, the very spy Cormac had just mentioned to Graham. Hamish was average height with an appearance so ordinary that he was immediately forgettable. The lad had a gift of blending into any crowd without ever once being noticed.

"Ye've got good news for us, aye?" Graham grinned with eager expectation, flashing the dimple on his right cheek. Cormac had a dimple on the opposite cheek, though it seldom made an appearance.

Cormac threw Graham a dark look, though in truth, he wished he could possess a similar optimism. Mayhap that might have been possible several months ago before the rain washed out their crops and almost all of their hope.

"I have news," Hamish said with obvious hesitation. "Their land doesna appear to be affected by the rains. No' like ours. But I dinna think they're likely to offer it to us."

"The MacDonalds?" Cormac surmised.

"Worse." Hamish grimaced. "The English."

"The English?" Graham echoed Cormac's disbelief.

"'Tis what is said around the towns." Hamish shrugged.

"Apparently Laird Ross's eldest sons have been promised to the daughters of English nobles. 'Tis said they'd inherit no' only lands at the border, but also considerable wealth."

Cormac considered what this might mean in relation to the number of grain stores. A wet chill blew in from the open window, spitting flecks of rain against Cormac's forearms where he'd pushed up his sleeves.

Hamish shifted his weight. "There's to be a jousting tournament in England. 'Tis where the unions are to take place."

"The daughters of English nobles, eh?" Graham's eyes twinkled in a way Cormac didn't like. "Where is this jousting tournament?"

Cormac frowned at his brother, but Hamish didn't appear to notice. "At the Rose Citadel, which they said is a days ride from the border."

"Daughters of English nobles with land near the border and considerable wealth," Graham repeated what Hamish had said and lifted his brows at Cormac.

Cormac eyed his brother warily. "I dinna like how ye're saying that."

"We could use considerable wealth," Graham said. "And the land on the border is far enough away to most likely no' be flooded like the lands here. Mayhap they'd have extra food."

Cormac grunted.

"We're fine-looking men." Graham gave his most charming smile and winked.

Cormac groaned aloud, already following where Graham's thoughts were heading. "Ye're no' going to the tournament to woo another man's lass."

Graham shot his brother a wounded look. "Nay, of course I'm no'." He rubbed his hands together with apparent anticipation. "We both are."

"Hamish, ye may take yer leave." Cormac crossed his arms over his chest, regarding his brother. "Nay."

"Think of it, Cormac." Graham hopped off the table and spread his hands wide. "If we both go, it'll double the chances of wooing at least one."

Cormac bristled. "I wouldna pin yer hopes on me."

"Maybe the lasses like grumpy men, eh?" Graham tilted his head in thought. "They are English after all."

"With all due respect, sir, 'tis a fair idea."

Cormac turned to find Hamish still standing by the door. How in God's teeth did the man stay so invisible?

"'Tis a terrible idea," Cormac countered.

Graham squared his jaw, as he often did when he'd stubbornly lodged his thoughts on a wild scheme. "Why?"

Cormac rattled through his thoughts, hating his inability to find a good reason. Aye, the lasses were promised to other men, and they might not want Cormac or Graham. Aye, it was wrong to try to steal a man's betrothed.

But it was far more wrong to let his clan starve.

Graham braced his palm against the wet window ledge and peered out to the rain-laden crops below. "Staying here willna fix this, Cormac."

"I know," Cormac muttered.

"And two of ye will have double the chance," Hamish piped up.

Cormac glared at him. "Take yer leave." This time Cormac didn't take his eyes from the man until the spy grudgingly slipped out and let the door close behind him.

"Ye know I'm right." Graham put a hand to Cormac's shoulder. "Ye just dinna like it."

Cormac heaved a great sigh of defeat. His brother was indeed correct on both accounts. It was the only viable plan on the horizon, and Cormac had spent countless hours puzzling how to save his clan with no real solution.

He closed the shutters and snapped them into place, abruptly cutting off the wind sweeping into the room and placing them in a darkness that took some getting used to. The meager candle on the desk glowed orange gold.

Cormac would do anything to spare his people another hungry winter. Even...flirt...possibly dance...with a woman who might care for another man.

Shite.

Then he thought of his childhood friend, Blair Sutherland, who had recently starved to death in an effort to feed his child. And of Ines Sutherland, whose sacrifice to others had also come at the cost of her life. And Ewan and Gregor as well as their mum. The list went on to include over two dozen of his people who had died from lack of food.

Cormac clenched his hand into a fist. His people looked to him to save them. He owed it to them, and to those who had died, to try to save them by any means possible. He steeled himself against the guilty stab of his morals. No matter what it took, no matter who he had to kill or rob or woo, he would ensure not one more Sutherland starved to death.

৩৯

Westmorland, England

THE VIAL OF POISON RESTED HOT AGAINST LADY ISOLDE Maxwell's palm.

She entered the solar and her brother, Gilbert Maxwell, Earl of Easton, lifted his head. "What do you want?"

They both shared the delicate appearance inherited from their late mother with slight figures, fair skin and sculpted cheekbones. But when Gilbert scowled as he did now, he resembled their father whose disposition had been equally as sour.

Isolde lifted her chin in silent refusal to be cowed by his usually foul demeanor. "You know why I'm here."

"Not this again." He pressed his hands to the smooth tabletop and regarded her with the impatient exasperation one does to a small child who fails at comprehension. "You are going to wed Brodie Ross of the Ross clan at Baron de la Rose's tournament this coming sennight." Gilbert had a slightly high pitch to his voice for a man, and when he spoke with such snideness, it took on a shrill tone.

"I do not wish to," Isolde replied, unwavering.

"But you will." Gilbert smiled coldly at her. "You haven't a choice."

"We don't need an alliance with the Ross clan." Isolde glanced around the opulent solar, which had become even more finely decorated after their miserly father's death. "We have a noble title, a good name and wealth enough to afford a comfortable life."

More than comfortable, in truth. Their life bordered on ostentatious now. The solar was only one example. The plain walls had been fitted with carved whorls and flowers along the tops of the walls and the fireplace, then painted with vivid color and gilt, so it practically glowed in the firelight. Gilbert had the great desk polished to a high shine and had commissioned several more pieces of furniture to be built, including two chairs before the hearth.

It was more than they needed. Especially when so many others had so little.

"You know why this must happen." Gilbert's statement took on a nasal condescension. "Your tattered reputation has need of salvaging."

Anger licked at her patience and heat simmered through her veins. "I did nothing wrong."

He gave a sharp bark of laughter. "If allowing a man liberties with your person and then refusing them marriage is not wrong, dear sister, I am uncertain what is."

She squeezed the vial in her hand. "I told you I was tricked."

"I know what you said." He steepled his long, slender fingers together. "And I know what I saw."

Isolde pressed her lips together. There was no use in arguing how she'd been found with Brodie in the hall, his body pinning her against the wall, her skirts pushed up to her thighs. Her cheeks burned now to even think of how exposed she'd been, how easily she'd been fooled. She'd been disgustingly naive.

Never again would she allow herself to be misled.

"You saw what he wanted you to," Isolde countered. "He feigned confusion as to where the Great Hall was located, bade me lead him there and then he pushed me against the stonework and hefted up my skirt so it would appear that..." Her words caught in her throat. She couldn't even speak of something so vile.

Her stomach writhed at the memory. He'd shoved her so hard that she'd smacked the back of her head on the whitewashed stones. She'd been too surprised to fight him off. By then, it was too late. Footsteps were headed in their direction, and his rough, callused hands were pushing up her skirt.

He hadn't actually touched her, thanks be to God. But the evidence of her naked leg, along with their improper proximity, had been enough to condemn her.

Her brother issued a flat smile. "Is that all, Isolde?"

The ire in Isolde's body made her blood as hot as boiling oil. "You told Mother you would look after me."

"Aye, but she's dead now." He narrowed his eyes. "And I made the promise before realizing you were such a slattern."

Isolde jerked back as though she'd been slapped. Indeed, she had been struck—deep in her chest and by the person who should care most for her in this world.

"I want you to cancel the arrangement for my union and instead fight Brodie to defend my honor." By some miracle, she was able to keep a quaver from her voice.

Gilbert cast his eyes to the ceiling with impatience. "Nay. We leave for the Rose Citadel in the morning."

All at once, she was glad she had found the courage to seek out the healer and procure the small vial. The potion wouldn't be enough to kill him. Isolde did not want him dead.

She did, however, need him to be unable to travel.

A night violently evacuating his bowels, and possibly the following day as well would leave him weak and in need of rest. Or so she'd been promised.

"Very well," Isolde said. "I'll be prepared."

It seemed like compliance, but in truth, they were the words she'd told her maid, Matilda, to listen for.

Gilbert did not notice that Isolde spoke slightly louder; he was simply eager for her acquiescence. His irritation melted away, and once more, he was her beautiful brother with a face that reminded her so fondly of her mother that it made her heart ache.

The door opened and Matilda entered with a flagon of wine and two chalices.

"I asked you to bring that a while ago," Isolde scolded. Though she and Matilda had planned the exchange, Isolde still loathed speaking so poorly to her trusted lady's maid.

"Forgive me, my lady." Matilda lowered her head in chastisement with such conviction that it made Isolde's chest squeeze.

She bit the inside of her cheek to keep from apologizing to her maid. "Leave the wine. I'll pour it."

"Aye, my lady." Matilda set the wine on a table across the room where Isolde would have to put her back to Gilbert to pour. With that, the maid bobbed a curtsey and quit the room.

"I apologize for the delay." Isolde indicated the flagon of wine. "Would you care for some wine before I go?"

Gilbert's gaze drifted to the table, and he licked his lips. "Aye."

His response had been expected. Gilbert never could resist the lure of wine. Just like their father. It turned him into the same man the late earl had been as well: impatient and ill-tempered.

Isolde faced the table and first poured herself a measure, then swiftly dumped the contents of the vial into the flagon. It was such a small amount, it made almost no sound as it married into the fine wine and the pale brown extract blended into the rich red without issue. She pretended to almost drop the flagon in an effort to churn the liquid together.

"You should have let your maid do it," Gilbert muttered.

"'Tis fine." Isolde splashed a hefty amount of wine into his goblet and carried both over to his desk, handing him the one with poison.

"To our mother." Isolde lifted her chalice.

"To our mother," Gilbert echoed. "And your impending nuptials."

Any regret Isolde may have harbored for what she was doing dissipated at that moment. She drank from her chalice as her brother swallowed down his wine with his usual zeal. No doubt it was nearly empty.

She watched his face carefully, fearing he might notice the sharp aftertaste of the purgative.

Gilbert drained his chalice without issue and got to his feet. "I've arranged for your belongings to be packed while we are at the tournament."

"Have you?" Isolde asked in a pleasant tone. After all, he would realize the futility of his plans within the hour. Perhaps sooner.

He fetched the flagon from the table and poured another helping. "Within a fortnight, you will be part of the Ross clan, dear sister, and we will have a strong ally in Scotland."

"Why do we need an ally in Scotland?" Isolde pulled her gaze from the wine in her brother's hand. The more he talked, the more he drank. And the more he drank, the more he talked.

And the sooner he'd consumed it all...

Gilbert scoffed at her as if she were too lacking to understand the reason. "The reason for an alliance with the Rosses is nothing for you to concern yourself over." He tilted the goblet back, as well as his head, while his neck flexed in a greedy swallow. His stare flicked to her goblet, and she knew he feared she might request more wine.

He had played right into her hands, predictably merciless against his vice.

She set her goblet on the edge of the desk. "I shall leave you to the rest of the wine." She smiled sweetly. "I want to ensure I have rested well before we travel to the Rose Citadel on the morrow."

Gilbert's shoulders relaxed, and he nodded. As though she needed his permission to leave. She departed without another word and made her way to her own chamber, where she found Matilda waiting. Their eyes met, and Isolde nodded in quiet conveyance that it had been done.

They passed the time together, finalizing their plans in whispered voices—the intent to leave in the middle of the night, taking everything Gilbert had packed for himself. He was just vain enough to remain home if he did not have his newly sewn fine clothes to wear. His armor would be coming with them as well, though it was not part of the plan to prevent him from following them.

Footsteps came from the solar below, frantic with the urgency of one's bowels about to erupt. Matilda and Isolde smothered their mirth as his bellows of exclamation filled the castle.

Nay, the armor was for Isolde. For if Gilbert refused to defend her honor, she would do it herself.

Travel from Scotland to England was a grueling journey spanning long, rain-soaked days that left Cormac in a terrible mood. At least finding the Rose Citadel had been relatively easy with all the ribbons and streamers dancing in the wind from the turrets like maypoles.

The brothers and two trusted clansmen, Duncan and Lachlan, dismounted amid the sea of tents and went about setting theirs among the others. Lucky for them, they'd all had the foresight to wrap their bags in the wax-coated linen tents to prevent everything they brought from being thoroughly soaked. They set up the tents with haste, eager to scour the travel from their skin and hair and wear dry clothes once more.

Duncan and Lachlan went to fetch some water for washing while Cormac and Graham tightened the last of the ropes. They were just finishing when a lanky man with messy brown hair approached. A medium-sized dog trotted at his side, its hair as matted and mud-colored as its owner's.

"Are you looking for a mercenary?" the man asked.

Cormac pulled the rope taut. "Nay."

The man rushed to secure the rope before Graham could help.

Cormac exchanged a glance with his brother before turning to the mercenary. "We're no' going to hire ye."

The man remained in place. "I don't see any mercenaries with you or any sort of guard. You'll have need of someone to mind your back."

Cormac braced his feet wide and looked down at the slender man who was a head shorter than he was. "I dinna think we do."

The dog issued a whine and stared up with soft brown eyes set beneath his filthy hair.

Was the dog begging Cormac now as well?

Cormac didn't bother to mention Duncan or Lachlan. Instead, he grabbed his pack and slipped into the tent with Graham following behind him.

"We dinna have time for all this," Cormac muttered. "No' when we have to prepare for the feast. We dinna even know what time it starts."

"Just before the sun goes down," the mercenary answered from outside the tent.

Cormac ignored the man's reply. Graham, however, called out to the man in thanks. Sundown was swiftly approaching. Not that they needed the motivation to hurry them from the wet clothes chafing at their skin. Duncan and Lachlan appeared several moments later with a bucket of fresh water to wipe away the mud of travel, while the brothers returned to their tent to prepare for the feast where they would be spying on the nobles.

Cormac and Graham changed into their finest tunics, which they belted over woolen hose, and emerged from the tent to discover the mercenary lounging outside, his back pressed to a pile of timber with his dog resting its head in his lap. The mercenary leapt up as his gaze caught Cormac and Graham.

"The feast is going to be one of the best from what I hear," the man said. "M'name's Alan and this here's Pip." The dog cocked his head at the mention, forehead rumpled with concentration.

"We dinna need an escort, Alan." Cormac fixed his gaze on the man. "We dinna need protection. Men already travel with us, men from our clan. Ye're no' wanted, and I'll no' be paying ye."

Not only did Alan appear nonplussed, but he also did not leave their side. "Do you even know where you're going?"

"The castle," Cormac replied. "Where I'll no' have need of ye."

"Aye, well, the entrance is that way." Alan indicated west with a long, thin finger. "You'll be going toward the back of the castle with the direction you're heading."

Cormac grudgingly shifted his direction.

"If you're not in the market for a mercenary, what are you here for?" Alan asked. "The joust? The melee? Revenge?" He stated the last word with dramatic flair, his brown eyes growing wide.

Graham met Cormac's gaze, and Cormac knew immediately what his brother was thinking. Neither of them knew what the ladies they sought looked like. Graham wanted to utilize the mercenary's knowledge of the people to glean the identities of the women.

Cormac shook his head, but Graham was already pressing a coin into Alan's palm and whispering in his ear. Alan nodded and picked up his pace with a determined purpose.

The Great Hall was packed with people by the time they entered. Musicians filled the air with the merriment of strings and pipes floating above the raucous din of too many conversations. A space would no doubt be cleared by the lower tables later for dancing.

Cormac grimaced at the idea of having to dance.

"There is Lady Clara de Montfort ," Alan said in a low whisper. "Daughter to the Norman Count de Evreux."

Cormac followed the direction of his stare to a brunette in a green kirtle with a pert smirk on her lips. She offered a chuckle to the woman next to her and casually sipped from the goblet in front of her.

"And there is Lady Isolde Maxwell." Alan shifted his focus across the capacious Great Hall. "Sister to Earl of Easton."

Cormac turned his head and stopped short. Lady Isolde wore a yellow silk gown that complimented her auburn hair and set her skin off like rich cream. Her face was delicate in its beauty with high cheekbones and finely arched brows, balanced with the fullness of her rosy lips.

Despite the excitement humming around her, Lady Isolde held only a small smile on her lips, as if she were offering it for posterity rather than in genuine enjoyment. She didn't engage in conversation with those around her, as others did. Nay, she gazed at the flowers strewn over the linen tablecloth with that plastered smile, her thoughts so far away, it made Cormac wonder where they took her.

Lady Isolde Maxwell.

Her name hummed in Cormac's veins like a challenge.

She was the lady he wished to woo. He regarded his brother, hoping beyond hope Graham would not seem as smitten by Lady Isolde as he.

But nay, Graham's focus was homed in on Lady Clara, a cocky grin already tipping the corner of his mouth.

Cormac leaned toward his brother. "Shall I take Lady Isolde?"

"And I'll help myself to Lady Clara." He lifted his brows suggestively and cut a path through the sea of people toward the Norman count's daughter.

Cormac was preparing in his mind what he planned to say to Lady Isolde when the nobleman at the dais, presumably Lord Yves, stood up and began a speech to welcome them all to the Rose Citadel.

"In case you aren't aware, he is Baron de la Rose," Alan said under his breath. "The man hosting the tournament. You can either sit here at the lower end of the table or outside with the servants."

Cormac lifted his brow. "I'm a chieftain."

THE HIGHLANDER'S LADY KNIGHT

"Then I leave you to your feast, my lord." Alan offered a slight bow and finally took his leave.

"'Tis 'sir,'" Cormac grumbled, but the man was already too far away to hear.

Cormac scanned over the crowd and once more found Lady Isolde. She was no longer bothering to feign a smile as she watched the baron deliver his welcome speech. Her eyes narrowed as if in contemplation, and Cormac found himself wishing to see what filled her thoughts. And what he might do to gain access to them. And through them—her.

A man appeared behind Lady Isolde and sank onto the bench beside her. Cormac bristled as he recognized the tall, blond beast of a man as none other than Brodie Ross, the Scotsman to whom Lady Isolde had been promised.

🕉

WHATEVER APPETITE ISOLDE HAD POSSESSED DISAPPEARED AS Brodie settled onto the bench next to her. The heat of his thigh settled against hers and made bile crawl up her throat.

"Good evening, my lady." His lowered voice held an intimacy she did not care for. Indeed, a shiver of disgust scrabbled over her flesh.

She did not bother to reply. She had hoped the empty seat at her side might be taken by another lord's daughter, although in the pit of her stomach, she'd anticipated it would be filled by Brodie.

Lord Yves's speech came to a conclusion, followed by cheers and toasts. Music and conversation resumed, and a servant settled a heavy platter of meat before them.

"We'll be married within a sennight." Brodie speared the venison with his eating dagger. "Lord Yves has already seen to all the preparations to ensure we can be wed following the melee."

He let the chunk of meat slide from his dagger onto her plate.

The cut was not a good one, riddled with fat that was already congealing into waxy white globs. For himself, he dug into the center of the pile of game and unearthed a slab of meat that still steamed with warmth from the oven.

Isolde swallowed the temptation to retch and glared down at her hands.

She wished she was wearing Gilbert's armor now so that she could throw the gauntlet at Brodie's feet and issue the challenge to save her honor. She was confident in her ability to fight with a sword. Her brother's Captain of the Guard, Hugh, had instructed her for several years after she'd been left alone in an attack at their home at Easton. She'd sworn then never to allow herself to feel so helpless and by God, she would honor that vow to herself now.

Brodie would not have her hand in marriage.

Once she was free from the obligation with Brodie, she'd leave the Rose Citadel and the whole foolishness of the tournament.

"Where is Lord Easton?" Brodie asked.

"My brother is supping in his rooms as he doesn't care for such formal occasions," Isolde replied curtly, having prepared the lie earlier on. Though it truly wasn't too far from the truth. While Gilbert enjoyed the glory and attention his title brought him, he didn't relish the tedium of ceremony or casual conversation with those he felt were beneath him. Had he not been ferociously ill the previous evening and still moaning in his chamber when Isolde left, he would no doubt be in the apartments upstairs with at least one comely lady ready to warm his bed.

Despite Gilbert's intention to wed Isolde off and the years of disdain he'd afforded her, she did experience a pinch of guilt for the incident with the potion. She'd even commissioned a stable lad to bring her word upon his recovery, so she could rest her conscience.

The feast dragged onward. Platters of food were set upon the linen table clothes among the scattered daisies and candles and salt cellars while wine and ale were poured liberally into goblets. Through it all, Brodie spoke to her as if she wished for his conversation. His diatribes were tedious in the faults he noted in others and offensive in the joy he took in such shortcomings.

Isolde pushed the food around on her fine metal plate, eager for it all to be done.

"Why's that Sutherland cur staring at ye?" Brodie asked abruptly.

Isolde lifted her head and caught sight of the man Brodie had referenced. He was taller than those sitting around him, his shoulders square and strong. He wore his dark hair to his shoulders and studied her with a fierce intensity he didn't bother to hide. Not even when she intentionally met his gaze to let him know that she noticed his attention.

Instead, he merely nodded once to her, as though in greeting. Unapologetic and bold and entirely unfamiliar.

She'd never seen the man in her life but didn't bother stating such to Brodie. It was none of his concern. Nothing in her life was any of his concern. And after she challenged him tomorrow and beat him in a fight, she would be free of the betrothal.

The beat of the music became somewhat faster, and several people stood from their benches to dance to the thrumming beat. Isolde bit into a honey cake, suddenly finding her appetite rather than be subjected to a dance with Brodie.

Not that he was so easily put off.

"Dance with me, Isolde." The tone of his voice didn't suggest a request so much as a demand.

She arched her brow at him and swallowed the bite of cake around her dry throat. "I did not give you leave to call me by my Christian name. You may address me as Lady Isolde."

He narrowed his eyes, then cleared away his irritated expression. "Dance with me, Lady Isolde."

"Nay." She turned away from him. "I won't wed you either, so do not set your heart on our union."

A hard grip curled around her forearm, hidden from sight by the tablecloth. "If ye keep talking with that stubborn tongue, I'll make sure ye're claimed thoroughly next time."

She wanted the hilt of a sword in her palm at that very moment, while facing him on the battlefield. Her muscles knotted with energy, eager for the opportunity to swing the heft of her blade and let it connect with jarring impact.

Instead, she jerked her arm free and stood. "Excuse me. I'm feeling rather unwell."

Matilda was at her side immediately.

A muscle worked in Brodie's jaw. Isolde thought he might protest her departure, but his small eyes scanned the nobles around them, several of whom had stopped to gape at him. He lowered his head reverently. "I bid you good evening, Lady Isolde."

She turned away from him and strode through the press of people with Matilda at her side.

"Will ye dance with me, Lady Isolde?"

The last thread of Isolde's nerves snapped. Civility and decorum were not worth the level of harassment she was receiving from the Scotsman.

"Nay." She spun on her heel to face Brodie. "And if you ask me once more, I'll—"

It was not Brodie who stood behind her, but the man who had watched her. Being in closer proximity to the curious stranger, she could make out the green of his eyes that had been indiscernible from a distance. He had a sharp jawline beneath the dark stubble he hadn't taken the time to shave. It was appealing, that shadow of coarse hair on his sculpted face.

He was appealing.

Far more than she liked to admit.

"Forgive me," she stammered. "I thought you were..." She shook her head. This man didn't need to know about her any more than Brodie did.

"I'm Cormac, Chieftain of the Sutherland Clan." He inclined his head rather than bowing.

"I'm Lady Isolde Maxwell," she replied.

"Well met." Sutherland shifted his weight from one foot to the other. "Would ye care to dance with me?"

She glanced toward the open space before the musicians. Brodie stood nearby with a group of men around him, some of whom were his brothers. There were five Ross lads in total, all at the Rose Citadel with their da, the Chieftain of the Ross clan. She'd heard from Matilda that Baston, the second eldest son, was set to marry a Norman count's daughter.

Isolde hated the Norman woman's fate as much as she hated her own. The whole lot of the Ross clan were bullies who relished the shame and pain of others for their own mirth. And if Isolde agreed to dance with the bold, mysterious Chieftain of the Sutherland clan, she would have to walk past the Rosses to do so.

What was more, if she danced with this man, Brodie would likely seek out Gilbert to discuss the offense. What would she do then? She couldn't very well meet privately with Brodie while wearing full armor with a helm to mask her identity.

"Forgive me, Sutherland," she said after a moment's hesitation. "My answer is still nay. Do excuse me." With that, she swept away with Matilda following closely behind her.

Mayhap it was rude of Isolde to leave him standing thus, but she could not risk jeopardizing her opportunity to challenge Brodie the following day. For it might be the only chance she would have to be free.

🙊 3 🙉

Cormac stood in silence for a heart-stopping moment as Lady Isolde strode away from him. Her narrow waist was displayed in her yellow silk kirtle, defined by a decorative gold belt and gilt thread had been plaited into her braid, so it glinted like stars in her fiery hair.

"You should have said please," Alan offered in a matter-of-fact tone.

Cormac frowned at him. "When did ye get back in here?" His frown deepened. "Where is Graham?"

Alan shrugged. "I figured you'd have need of my assistance."

Cormac grunted.

Alan lifted his chin expectantly.

"Verra well," Cormac growled in frustration. "Where is Graham?"

"With Lady Clara." Alan scratched Pip on the head, stopped and pinched a flea between his nails.

Agitation tensed at the back of Cormac's neck. Graham always knew what to say to women. It was Cormac who could handle the many tasks and tedious details of being chieftain. But

Graham was the charismatic one who knew what to say and how to say it.

"Do you need advice with Lady Isolde?" Alan asked in a tone that was almost pompous.

Cormac didn't like it. But he was also desperate.

In the distance, Lady Isolde was making her way to the exit. If he hurried, he could still catch her.

"Fine," Cormac said with exasperation. "Tell me what to say to her."

"Tell her she's lovely and ask her nicely to dance with you." Alan lifted a shoulder as if what he was suggesting was an obvious solution. "Mayhap follow your request with a 'please.'"

But Cormac didn't respond; he was already pushing through the throngs of colorfully dressed nobles to where Lady Isolde was nearly to the great double doors that would lead her out of the Great Hall and ruin his chance to make a better impression.

"Lady Isolde," he called.

She didn't stop.

Be polite.

"Forgive me, Lady Isolde," he tried again.

This time she did stop and turn toward him. Her brows furrowed. "Sutherland, was there something you needed?"

Aye. A massive fortune and land nearby with food enough to feed his people through the winter.

"I dinna think I asked ye right the first time." He tried to mimic Graham's charming smile.

Her brows pinched closer together.

"I think ye're quite bonny," he said.

"Bonny?" She repeated the word as if she found it unfamiliar.

But then, she would be as it was a word more often used in Scotland.

He cleared his throat. "It means lovely. Ye're verra bonny with a fine..." Panicking somewhat, he let his gaze skim down her body.

It immediately rested on her firm breasts, the generous swell visible from the top of her gown. "...bosom."

The lady's maid gave a little squeak, and Lady Isolde's eyes went wide.

Shite.

"I dinna mean that." He put his hands out, as though he could physically stop the conversation. God, he wished such a thing were even possible. "I mean, I do. Ye've got fine breasts, but I dinna mean—" He dropped his hands in defeat. "Would ye dance with me?" He grimaced. "Please."

She blinked up at him. "Nay, but I thank you for the offer."

He nodded, not blaming her a bit. God's teeth, he'd mucked that one up.

Her eyes lit up all at once. "Is this your dog?"

"Aye," he answered quickly.

Alan's eyes went wide with alarm, and Cormac immediately regretted his swift reply.

Lady Isolde knelt on the rushes and instructed her maid to procure some meat for the beast. She worked her fingers into the dog's fur behind his ears and scratched until one of his hind legs began to itch at the air. She laughed and handed him a bit of meat from her maid before standing upright once more.

The elation at meeting Pip faded from her eyes. "You should care for your pet properly, Sutherland. The poor thing is thin as a skeleton and covered in dirt and fleas."

Cormac's skin went hot at the chastisement. He should never have claimed the dog as his own.

"Good evening, Sutherland." This time when Lady Isolde departed with her lady's maid, Cormac did not try to go after her.

"Pip isn't for sale." Alan's jaw was clenched with determination. "I'd never sell him. Not for all the coin in England."

"He's yers," Cormac confirmed. "But I'd like ye to ensure he's bathed and fed." He surveyed the mercenary. "Ye too."

Alan held out his palm.

Cormac sighed and dug out his purse. This lie about the dog being his was by far one of the most foolish ones he'd told. He set a coin in Alan's hand.

"And you'll only pretend he's your dog," Alan said slowly.

Cormac nodded.

The mercenary gave a more relaxed smile, picked up Pip and carried him from the Great Hall to comply with Cormac's request. At least that was one small task seen to. The following day, he would have to smooth over what he had so terribly ruffled today with Lady Isolde.

He hoped Graham was having a better time with Lady Clara, as Cormac didn't hold much confidence in his own ability to woo Lady Isolde. Especially when he'd had such a terrible start.

☙❧

ISOLDE'S STOMACH TWISTED IN A SERIES OF ANXIOUS KNOTS. The nervous energy humming through her veins left her restless, but she forced herself to remain still while Matilda dressed her in the heavy chainmail and surcoat.

It had taken her maid a fortnight of finding excuses to be around the guards to learn how to get all the straps and buckles fastened correctly. Now, she implemented that knowledge with fingers made deft through the days of practice they'd run through before leaving for the Rose Citadel.

Matilda finished securing the blue-and-white surcoat over the chainmail and regarded Isolde with a worried crinkle to her otherwise smooth brow. "Are you certain this is safe, my lady?"

Isolde shoved aside the fear trying to edge into her resolve. "It most assuredly is not safe, but I cannot marry Brodie."

Matilda's large gray eyes reflected her concern. "What if—?"

Isolde shook her head vehemently. "Do not say it. Don't even think about it. We must be confident. Without a doubt."

Matilda nodded and pressed her lips together, as though

sealing away her misgivings. She lifted the bucket-shaped helm, and Isolde's world went dark as it fit over her head. A thin band of vision showed before Isolde's eyes but little else. It wasn't ideal, of course, but it was necessary to hide her identity.

"I shall return posthaste," Isolde said in a lofty tone, imitating the nasal speech of her brother.

Matilda's worry dissolved into a grin. "You're almost too good at that."

"Impossible," Isolde snipped. "Remain here and cover for my wayward sister while I defend her honor as I should have done weeks ago."

Matilda offered an exaggerated curtsy. "As you wish, my lord."

Isolde straightened her back and strode from the room, not only adorned in Gilbert's armor but also his pompous arrogance. She located the practice field on the outskirts of the sea of tents without difficulty. It was easy when one followed the clangs, clatters and grunts. Locating Brodie, however, would be far more challenging around so many men.

She strode through the crowd, searching with her obstructed vision. To no avail.

"Are you looking for someone?" The lanky man who had been with Sutherland the night before put himself into her line of sight. His brown hair had been combed and gleamed cleanly in the early morning light.

"Brodie Ross," Isolde answered in her brother's petulant tone. "Have you seen him?"

The man shook his head. "The Chieftain of the Sutherland clan is getting ready to practice with several men. Perhaps you'd like to join them while you wait?"

He indicated a gathering of several Scotsmen in armor. Sutherland was easy to identify with his height and the breadth of his shoulders. Something bumped at Isolde's knee. She glanced down to find a dog nudging at her for attention. Not just any dog, this was the one belonging to Sutherland, now so thoroughly washed she could see that the muddy hair was actually a shiny buttery gold.

Sutherland had taken her advice. She didn't bother to hide her smile, knowing it couldn't be seen under her helm. She did, however, smooth her gloved hand over the dog's head. The beast gazed up at her with adoration, its pink tongue lolling from the side of its mouth.

"Alan, are ye inviting people to join us?" Sutherland frowned at the man, evidently displeased.

It was on the tip of Isolde's tongue to decline the invite, but then she remembered she was pretending to be her brother. And Gilbert would never be so charitable. Besides, some light combat might help ease some of the tension roiling through her body. As it was, her blood pumped through her veins with such force that she felt ready to burst.

"I could use the practice," she said in Gilbert's lofty tone.

Sutherland slid her a wary glance.

"He evens out our number," a red-haired man wearing no surcoat over his chainmail said.

Sutherland didn't answer so much as he simply grunted, but it appeared to be acquiescence enough. Isolde joined the men as two others prepared for a mock fight against one another.

"Do ye always walk about with yer helmet on?" Sutherland kept his own head bare as he braced for combat.

"I didn't pay a king's fortune for this armor to not wear it," Isolde said, plucking her brother's words without effort.

Sutherland scoffed. "I'm sure ye dinna get the chance often to wear it in battle. At least no' outside of tournaments and practice."

Isolde simply raised her sword rather than deign to reply. Sutherland didn't move toward her. No doubt, he knew her—or rather her brother's—arrogance and was assured she would advance first. And advance she did, with her blade aggressively swiping toward him.

He evaded the strikes, shifting this way and that, his movements smooth. When she lowered her weapon to prepare to strike once more, he took advantage and jabbed at her side, a blow she only just managed to dodge. It was then she knew she had to forego her brother's overconfidence on the field lest she fall. In this one thing, she would rely on her own education and instinct, lest she end up dead.

"Do ye think that bonny serving wench will be at our table again tonight, Duncan?" the red-haired man asked.

His opponent, a man with cropped dark hair, grinned. "Ach, I hope so. She had a fine set of duckies on her."

Isolde's face burned with mortification at the man's crude speech about the woman's breasts. Her own were bound tightly beneath a band of linen. It was a necessary discomfort she would gladly endure for an opportunity to defeat Brodie Ross.

Sutherland shot a long-suffering look at the two men.

Duncan held up his free hand in surrender. "I canna help that I noticed she was a fine thing to gaze upon. And ye're one to chastise when ye were talking up the bonny lass in the yellow kirtle."

Isolde froze, uncertain if she ought to interrupt this discussion lest her own "duckies" be put on the table for discussion. After all, Cormac had made a point of noting his appreciation for them the night before.

"Blundering, more like." Sutherland's mouth quirked in a smile and a dimple showed in his left cheek. "Lady Isolde is too fine a lass for the likes of me."

The men laughed.

"Lady Isolde?" she haughtily quipped. "I say, that's my sister you're referring to. You haven't come to speak to me of any interest."

Sutherland turned his glare first to Alan, who offered an apologetic smile, then to her as his eyes narrowed with skepticism. "With all due respect, if I had an interest in the lady, I'd converse with her rather than her brother."

Heavens. What a perfect response.

"I'm in charge of what she does," Isolde countered, testing Sutherland further. "No man can consider her without my permission. And if you want her for marriage, you better offer me a pretty fortune."

Sutherland's expression turned to one of barely concealed disgust. "She's a lass. No' cattle." He lifted his sword. "Enough of this banter, let's do what we came to do and warm our muscles with practice, aye?"

Isolde was glad she wore the helm, lest he see the awed expression on her face. No man had ever spoken in such a manner to her brother. Certainly, Gilbert would never have allowed it. But she was the puppeteer controlling her brother's image, and she would do nothing to sway such glorious ideals.

She lifted her weapon and tried to put Sutherland from her thoughts so she could more readily focus.

After all, he had suddenly become quite fascinating.

♞ 4 ♘

I solde fought several rounds with Sutherland and one with Duncan, and the other man whose name she learned was Lachlan. She beat both the men and won two of the five sets with Sutherland.

Her body hummed with energy, now properly adjusted to the weight of the chainmail, so it was more comfortable than hindering. Even her muscles seemed to glide through her movements, lubricated with the heat of practice.

She turned to face Duncan once more and stilled. There, emerging from a tent just behind her opponent, was one of the Ross brothers. Where there was one, there were often several. Her heartbeat tripled in her chest.

The force of Duncan's body slammed into her, knocking her down. She scrambled upright and pushed him away with one hand. Her helm had been knocked askew by the impact and the world careened in the narrow slit, shoved far to the right. She put her gloved palms to the metal and adjusted it as she searched frantically through the view.

There were more people now. Too many. She searched all their faces.

"Lord Easton?" Duncan asked.

Isolde put her hand up to stop him. "I'm looking for someone."

As she spoke in her brother's snide tone, her gaze landed on a beast of a man with long blond hair. Brodie. Ire rose in her, molten with the power of her success in practice. She would fight him now. She would defeat him and be victorious.

She would be free.

With her stare locked on him, she strode in his direction.

Brodie wore a red-and-white surcoat belted over his chain-mail, his gait confident. He grinned as she approached. "Good morrow, Lord Easton."

Isolde didn't bother to return the sentiment. Gilbert wouldn't have. "I release you from your contract to wed my sister."

"I dinna want to be released." Brodie's pleasant expression darkened. "We had an agreement."

"Nay," Isolde snapped. "You decided to lay hands on my sister and force the issue of your union."

Brodie's brows furrowed and he appeared...well, he appeared rather confused. Caution rattled around in her brain like a stone.

"It was yer idea," Brodie said in a low voice, his brow puckered with disbelief. "Ye set the whole thing up."

Disgust curdled low in her belly. It was no wonder Gilbert refused to defend her honor, when it had been his hand that shifted the pieces to ruin Isolde's life.

"I've changed my mind," Isolde said.

"Ye canna do that," Brodie growled.

"I just did." Isolde spun away, but even as she did so, she knew he would not accept Gilbert's change of heart so readily.

"Lord Easton," he barked.

Isolde turned back to him, and a knot drew tight and hard in her chest.

"We had an arrangement," Brodie said. "And I'll no' let ye back out of what we'd agreed to. I will wed yer sister."

What had been arranged? She hated not knowing what her brother had received in return for her freedom. She hated even more that she couldn't ask without completely giving herself away.

"You will not wed her," Isolde countered.

"Now ye try to renege?" Brodie spat on the ground before Isolde's feet, and for the first time, she found herself glad for her limited visibility, which prevented her from having to see the offending foam in the trampled grass in front of her.

"Ye got what ye wanted," Brodie said in a low snarl. "And I'll have what I'm owed."

Helpless frustration bunched at the muscles along the back of her neck. What had Gilbert already received from Brodie?

She ripped the gauntlet off her hand and glared up at Brodie through her helm. Without another word, she threw it hard at his feet. The impact rattled metal where finger and wrist joints met each other in a clatter.

Brodie lifted a bushy brow.

"I challenge you, Brodie Ross," Isolde said in a loud, clear voice. "In defense of my sister's honor."

As she spoke, she tried to keep her hand curled into a fist at her side. While she might be of similar height and stature to her brother and possess the ability to alter her voice like his, she could do nothing about the femininity of her long, slender fingers.

"I accept yer challenge." Brodie sneered down at her. "For ye have no honor, ye lying English whoreson."

Anticipation jolted through Isolde. She jerked her sword free, ready to battle where they stood.

Brodie chortled. "No' now. I'll be jousting by and by and need practice." He shook his head as though she was of little concern. "On the morrow, aye?"

Disappointment rained down on her. "Very well," she conceded. "On the morrow."

"Enjoy yer last day of living." He smirked.

Isolde bit back a retort. Brodie stalked away without glancing back. She waited until the crowd swallowed him before she lifted her gauntlet from where it laid in the dirt and slid it back over her hand.

The blow of not being able to take Brodie on at that moment was a difficult one to stomach. She uttered a vulgar curse she'd heard men use before. Surprisingly, the coarse language aided somewhat in ebbing her frustration.

And her impatience need not nip at her long. On the morrow, she would have her vengeance and her freedom. Several couriers walked by wearing their finery, a reminder she too was expected to be present at the parade and the jousting later on that day.

She buried her frustration and shifted her direction to return to the castle so Matilda could prepare her for the parade. Sutherland stood several paces away, his attention fixed fully on her, having witnessed the entire exchange. Far too interested.

She recalled his request for a dance. Twice.

Discontent added a new level of sourness to her already churning gut. For it was apparent that gaining her freedom from one man might place her back in the focus of another.

Aye, she would do well to avoid Sutherland.

৩❀৩

LATER THAT MORNING, ON HIS WAY TO THE PARADE, CORMAC glanced at the attendees for Lady Isolde. Hoping no one noticed, he tugged at the stiff tunic he wore over a scratchy pair of hose. Both were new and viciously uncomfortable. He loathed having to wear such finery, but one couldn't capture the attention of an earl's sister with the simple tunics and hose he usually wore, ones that had been softened by age. And faded by it as well, unfortunately.

He paused mid-stride and tried pulling at the fabric at his thighs to dislodge his braies from where they were firmly wedged between his buttocks. Except his hands slid off the slick fabric of the tunic and the hose pinched in his grasp for just long enough to ride higher, bringing the braies another inch with it.

Shite.

"With all due respect," Alan said in a low tone. "You're walking like you've got something shoved up your arse."

Cormac glared at him. "I've got half my braies up there if ye must know."

Alan grimaced.

Cormac tried to set his unease from his mind and scanned the moving crowd before him once more. People of all ages and classes blended together into the mix of wealthy and poor, the former donned in resplendent finery while the latter was freshly scrubbed and in their best clothes. All moved together in their haste to witness the parade.

Finding Lady Isolde through the mix of veils, hoods and felted hats seemed a near-impossible task. Until Pip went bounding off into the sea of people.

"Stop, Pip," Alan exclaimed as he took off after the dog.

Cormac reveled in the brief moment of silence with the two gone and was once more reminded of the braies invading his arse. What was the point of wealth if it made someone so utterly miserable?

Alan came into view in the near distance, along with Pip, who sat at a woman's feet and gazed up at her with adoration.

Lady Isolde.

She wore her long hair coiled into a delicate gold caul dotted with pearls. Her gown was a lovely sky blue that accented her fair, flawless skin. She beamed down at Pip with a sweet expression of joy that curved at her full lips to reveal two straight rows of teeth.

She glanced up when he arrived and inclined her head. "Sutherland."

"Good morrow, Lady Isolde." He offered her a smile he hoped

came across as charming as his brother's. Being a twin, he knew it looked good on Graham. On him, however, it felt rather foolish.

"We washed Pip for you." Alan beamed at her, clearly seeking her approval.

"Aye, I saw earlier." Color rose in Lady Isolde's cheeks. "Earlier, I mean, when he ran toward us moments ago."

The woman at her side, a comely brunette in simpler clothes, nodded.

"We can walk to the stands together." Cormac offered Lady Isolde his arm. "I'll join ye in watching the parade."

She stiffened and did not take his proffered arm.

"Ask her," Alan mouthed from behind Lady Isolde.

Cormac bit the inside of his cheek to keep from rolling his eyes. "If ye'd allow me to join ye, that is."

She hesitated, then opened her mouth and paused again. "Aye," she said at last and slid her hand into the crook of his arm. "Are you not jousting today?"

"I'm no' here to joust." Cormac navigated the crowd of people and tried to use his body to prevent her from being jostled.

She tilted her head up at him. Sunlight streamed over her face and made her blue eyes glow, reflecting flecks of pale green in their depths. "Why are you here, then?"

"At the joust?" He edged them around a tall man who lumbered onward without any haste.

"At the tournament," she replied.

To find ye. To wed ye and steal ye from the man who never deserved ye.

"To find a mercenary." He slid a look at Alan.

Alan straightened beside him and gave a wide, beaming smile.

Cormac suppressed a groan and irritably shifted his attention from the unwanted mercenary who had weaseled his way into a job.

The crowd squeezed into the small area funneling them toward the stands. Lady Isolde shifted closer against Cormac's side. "Then you'll be leaving soon?" she asked. "Now that you've found a mercenary, I mean."

"Nay, I dinna plan to," Cormac answered, nonplussed.

"He's fighting in the melee for his clan on Friday, my lady," Alan piped up.

Cormac narrowed his eyes, but Alan nodded encouragingly in an apparent effort to help Cormac come up with a sufficient excuse to remain at the tournament.

"The melee." Isolde lifted her slender brows. "I hear it will be filled with strong competition."

"You've heard that because Cormac is the best," Alan supplied.

This time, Cormac scowled at the man he'd just hired and might soon let go.

Alan put up his hands and fell back a step, finally going quiet.

Cormac caught sight of Brodie Ross in the crowd and the desire to protect Lady Isolde tightened through him. There was no question in his mind that Brodie had seen them as well. Brodie glared at Isolde's hand tucked against Cormac's arm, his anger palpable.

Cormac ignored his rival intentionally and led Lady Isolde into the wooden stands where her maid sat to one side of her and he at the other, along with Alan, while Pip lay at her feet. A stream of knights then entered amid a bellow of cheers as the sun glinted off their polished armor and the banners around them rippled in a rainbow of color.

After the parade of knights came Lord Yves once more as he and another man made an announcement welcoming them all to the tournament, followed by a list of rules and the blaring of trumpets. Two knights readied themselves on opposing sides of the stretch of land in front of the stands and the joust began.

Several moments later, Lady Isolde turned her face away as the men raced toward one another, their lances locked firmly in their grips. One smashed into a knight in an explosive impact that showered both riders in splinters of wood. Lady Isolde gave a little start and closed her eyes.

"Do ye no' like the joust?" Cormac asked.

Lady Isolde kept her gaze from the field. "Nay. 'Tis too violent. I cannot abide by the weapons or men being struck by them." She shivered.

"Yer brother doesna share yer disdain for such things." Cormac glanced around in the stands to see if the earl was in attendance. "I'm surprised he's no' here. He seemed eager for a fight this morning."

"He doesn't care for formal events such as these." Lady Isolde's face shifted in Cormac's direction. "You saw my brother this morning?"

Cormac nodded. "Aye, I practiced a few rounds with him. And he issued a challenge."

The field in front of them was cleared and the next pair of men began to prepare for their joust.

Lady Isolde lifted a slender eyebrow upward. "What did you think of his skill?"

"He's a skilled fighter," Cormac replied. "His moves are deft and executed well."

"What else?" she pressed.

He shifted in his seat, suddenly leery of saying more.

She gave him a coy smile that teased at something in his chest. "Are you holding something back?"

Cormac swallowed. "I feel he could benefit from more physical strength."

She frowned, evidently offended.

An ache at his temples thundered to life. Why in God's teeth did he have to be so terrible at wooing women?

"Do you think he can prevail with this challenge he issued?" she asked.

This time he considered his reply before opening his mouth. "I hope so. After all, the challenge is for yer honor."

5

I solde's face went hot at the mention of her honor and its need to be protected. When she'd been playing the part of Gilbert, she hadn't once considered how she would react to knowledge of his challenge from her own perspective.

Now, however, it mortified her to have something so private be aired so publicly.

Sutherland shifted in his seat. "I've made ye uncomfortable."

Nay, I have.

"It isn't you." Isolde shook her head. "I...forgive me, I fear I cannot watch another joust. If you'll excuse me..."

"Aye, of course." He got to his feet to help her to hers, which she acknowledged with a polite nod of thanks.

"Sit down," someone hissed from behind Isolde.

Sutherland shot a glare over his shoulder, and whoever had been complaining went quiet. Isolde moved quickly to avoid blocking anyone else's view.

In truth, she enjoyed tourneys. The jousts were always her favorite, filled with excitement, uncertainty and fascinating rivalries. It was curious how such rivalries began. Some started with the simplest misunderstandings that turned friends to enemies, some were borne of violence, and others still dated so far back in time no one could remember the origin.

Isolde went down the stairs with Matilda behind her and paused behind a column near the stands to watch as the two knights collided into one another. The lance of the knight closest to her shattered against the chest of his opponent, shoving him back with such force, he was thrown from his horse. Isolde clapped at his victory. Not only had he won the round, but he had also won the other knight's horse.

Before Isolde could be drawn into another round of jousting, she and Matilda quit the tournament fields and swiftly strode toward the Rose Citadel. It was not yet noon, and already her day had been trying.

She quickened her pace as they neared the tents. Even with Matilda at her side, Isolde knew well to avoid the tented area where the knights were roughened by competition and made bold by inflated bragging.

A hand shot out and clamped around her arm, pulling her into the shadows.

Another man, a blond-haired Ross brother, locked Matilda in his arms and put a dirk to her throat.

"If ye scream, Garret will slit her throat." Brodie's voice rasped in Isolde's ear, his breath sour with ale.

Isolde forced herself to remain still.

Brodie spun her around, his eyes narrow slits of hatred. "I saw ye making a fool of me with the chieftain of the Sutherland clan. Did ye pressure yer brother to challenge me?" He scoffed. "Honor, indeed. I'll make sure there's no honor left to salvage."

His free hand roughly grabbed her hips, and she knew well what he meant. She could fight him off, she knew. Matilda, however, was not so well-trained.

Isolde took some comfort in the dagger strapped to her belt. If she could discreetly grasp the hilt, she could throw it at Garret and injure him, then attack Brodie. It was the best option to keep Matilda safe while protecting herself as well.

Her fingertips hadn't even had time to crawl toward the dagger when Brodie heaved a grunt and jerked to the side with her still clutched in his arms. She crashed to the ground in a bone-jolting slam. It wasn't the first time in her life she'd been thrown hard enough to knock the wind from her lungs. Hugh had taught her well, and that included landing hard blows when necessary to teach her basic skills for survival. As a result, she was comfortable with keeping her wits about her in combat.

She yanked the dagger from her belt and scrambled upright, away from Brodie, with the blade pointed in his direction. The effort was not needed.

Sutherland sat atop Brodie and pulled his arm back to slam into Brodie's face. He had no need of her aid. But Matilda...

Isolde spun on her heel to find Garret frozen with indecision. Before she could step toward her maid to help, a snarling beast raced toward Isolde and planted himself in front of her as a wiry man tackled Garret to the ground.

Though half the Highlander's size, Alan nimbly forced the larger man into the dirt and put a dagger to his throat, his usual congenial expression coldly devoid of any emotion. "If it weren't for Sutherland's order not to kill you, you'd be dead." Alan jerked his hands at Garrett's shoulders. "Especially since you are a man who would try to take advantage of unprotected ladies."

Pip growled again and took a menacing step toward Garret as if backing the mercenary's claims.

The fleshy smack of a fist striking skin came from behind Isolde, where Sutherland and Brodie fought.

Brodie grunted. "Leave us be, Sutherland. I've no qualms with ye."

She glanced over her shoulder to where they wrestled on the ground.

"I have qualms with ye assaulting a lady." Sutherland drew his arm back to strike again.

"She's my betrothed." Brodie writhed under Sutherland, trying to free himself from being pinned to the ground. "What I do with the lass is no' any of yer concern."

Sutherland's fist smashed into Brodie's nose, which gave a sickening crunch. Brodie howled in agony, and Sutherland finally pushed himself off the other man. He didn't wait to ensure Brodie was still down.

Instead, he immediately went to Isolde. Sutherland hovered near her, as though uncertain if he ought to reach for her. In the end, he folded his arms awkwardly over his chest and leaned in close, protective proximity of her.

Isolde couldn't help the flash of disappointment. Part of her craved those strong arms wrapping around her, keeping her safe. Giving her comfort. Another part of her, admittedly a much smaller part, knew it was inappropriate to wish for such intimate nearness with him.

"Were ye injured?" Sutherland asked.

"Nay." She looked to her maid, but Matilda shook her head, her hands clutched together over her chest.

Sutherland's squared shoulders didn't lower. "Alan, release the bastard. Let him help his brother to a healer."

Brodie cursed from where he lay on the ground, hand cupped over his bleeding nose. Alan pulled back from Garret, who scrambled to his feet and raced over to Brodie.

"Ye'll pay for this, Sutherland." Brodie's words were muffled by his bloody hand at his face.

Sutherland didn't deign to acknowledge the threat. He kept his gaze fixed on Isolde, concern evident in his dark green eyes. She was struck once more with how handsome a man he truly was, with his square jaw now scraped clean of whiskers and a straight nose.

"May I walk ye to the castle?" he offered.

This time, Isolde didn't hesitate. Her fingers slid into the strong warmth in the crook of his arm. A tremor rattled through her body, one swept by a wave of emotions: the fear for what could have happened, the relief for emerging unscathed, the appreciation for Sutherland's assistance and the apprehension for what would come in the future. Her knees were soft beneath her weight, and it was all she could do to keep from allowing herself to melt against the support of his solid body.

"Mayhap it isna my place to say this..." He spoke in a slow, careful tone. "But I dinna think yer betrothed is worthy of ye."

Heat singed Isolde's cheeks. "I never agreed to marry him."

She stopped when they reached the entrance of the castle. "I'm fine from here. Thank you for your aid."

His brow furrowed, and she knew he was not yet finished with their conversation. "Is this why yer brother challenged Brodie over yer honor?"

She looked away. A row of red banners rippled in the wind like forked tongues. "Thank you for bringing me to the castle—"

"I'd like to speak with Lord Easton," Sutherland said.

"You may find him bantering among the men preparing to joust, though he will not be participating himself. It never was his sport." She inclined her head, cutting off the conversation before Sutherland could pry any more. "Good day to you, Sutherland."

He offered no further protest. Isolde and Matilda climbed the stone staircase to their private chambers. Only then did Isolde allow her legs to collapse. She flopped onto her mattress and put a hand over her racing heart.

"Are you well, my lady?" Matilda asked.

Isolde stared up at the green linen trappings hanging over the bed. "After the fight tomorrow, we need to be prepared to leave."

"I'll have everything at the ready," her maid assured her.

But the tension did not drain from Isolde's shoulders. Not when Sutherland had injected himself so completely into her mind, not when so much was riding on the fight tomorrow. And certainly not when fear nipped at the back of her mind, plaguing her with terrifying doubt.

⚜

After Cormac had defeated Brodie, he'd sent Duncan and Lachlan to keep an eye on the brothers while Alan went to glean gossip from the ranks. Following an unsuccessful attempt to locate the Earl of Easton, Cormac had taken the time to bathe in the chilly loch. Even as he made his way to the Rose Citadel that night for the feast with Alan and Pip, his hair was still slightly damp, but his body was invigorated with the chill of the water, and all the remnants of travel swept away.

Additionally, he was more confident in where he stood with Lady Isolde's favor. Or at least, more so than he had been previously. Alan had once more proven his worth in obtaining invitiations for them into the castle that evening, a feast meant only for the castle guests and special attendees by invite-only. Cormac navigated through the crowd of tournament attendees and scanned the head table, seeking out Lord Easton. Cormac's inability to locate the man left him vexed. Who would betroth their sister to such a man as Brodie Ross from the first? And why was Lord Easton now issuing a challenge over Lady Isolde's honor? And why was he so damnably hard to locate?

Cormac meant to unearth the answers to his questions that eve, for he knew somehow in doing so, he would identify the key to Lady Isolde's heart. Or mayhap such a thought was simply him hoping.

His gaze fell upon Lady Isolde, and Pip scampered off in her direction.

Alan gazed after his pet. "You keep him tonight. He'll get finer eating in the hall than outside with the servants." He winked. "Besides, he's your dog."

Cormac opened his mouth to reply, but then Lady Isolde's

gaze went from Pip up to search the sea of people. For him. She was looking for him.

Cormac nodded. "Remember what we discussed."

Alan was to seek out any information he could find on Brodie Ross. Or any of the Ross brothers. The jousters had provided no information of use, and Duncan and Lachlan had not found any serviceable information either.

Alan straightened, like a soldier who'd been issued orders. "Aye, I'll uncover what I can."

Cormac nodded at the man and wound through the Great Hall to where Lady Isolde sat at the high table.

"May I sit with ye?" he asked. In truth, he would have just sat down, but Alan had informed him it was preferable to give a lady a choice in the matter. "Please."

"Aye, ye may." Lady Isolde smiled up at him, a beautiful glowing expression that lit the darkest regions of his soul. God's teeth, the lass was so bonny.

Pip had already taken a place under the table at her feet, his eager brown gaze lifted in expectation of any food that might fall to him.

Cormac sank onto the bench beside her. Immediately a serving wench approached with a tankard of ale for him.

He glanced about, finding naught but an old woman with feathery white hair at Isolde's other side. "Where is Lord Easton this night?"

Her smile faltered. "Most likely taking his meal in his private chamber. He is not one for feasts."

Steaming plates of food were set before them, great platters of venison and fowl along with more bread than Cormac had ever seen before in his life. He could only imagine delivering such a bounty of food to his own people.

Most of the men around him had belts that strained at the girth of their waists. An indication they feasted so luxuriously with regularity. That past winter, over a dozen of the Sutherland clan had perished from starvation. It was a terrible death, with one's stomach so empty and their bodies wasted away to the skeleton.

Cormac had been there to help bury them, those slender bodies that weighed too little. He knew all of their stories and had carved every one of their names into his heart, a burden he would never cease to carry.

And here the nobility supped, belching through greasy mouths, reaching for more though their need for food had been sated.

They did not know true hunger.

"Are you well?" Lady Isolde asked.

Cormac blinked. "Aye."

"Whatever were you thinking about?" She queried.

He shook his head, not willing to speak of his people's plight. And how terribly he'd failed them.

For he had failed them. In the most awful of ways.

"I tried to locate Lord Easton earlier." He took a fat cut of pheasant with juicy white meat and golden-crisped skin, the best piece he could find, and set it on the plate in front of Lady Isolde.

She allowed him to do so and thanked him. "Did you find my brother, then?"

Cormac cut another piece from the pheasant, his knife piercing the browned, roasted skin, then slicing easily through the tender meat beneath. It was a far more generous portion than he allowed himself back home.

"I couldna find yer brother," Cormac confessed. "I searched through the waiting knights as well as the stands and tents. All to no avail."

She gave a little hum of acknowledgment and took a dainty bite of meat.

"Why did he promise ye to Brodie Ross?" Cormac asked.

Her brows flinched together, and he knew the question put her off.

"I hear the melee on Friday will be one of the grandest in England," she said in a casual tone.

He didn't question the change in topic any more than he did the light conversation she kept up through the meal. She commented on the food and several of the jousters she'd heard who had been successful that day. Everything she said steered away from any personal details of herself or her brother. Such omissions were indeed noticed.

Still, he enjoyed the manner in which she spoke, how she noted things others might not and injected a bit of humor into details. And through it all, she'd slipped bites of meat down to Pip, who eagerly caught them in his sharp little teeth before they could land in the rushes.

At last, the plates were cleared, and the tables at the other end of the Great Hall were set aside to make room for dancing.

Lady Isolde's gaze was fixed fully on him, wide blue eyes lashed with sable, her lips lifting slightly at the corners in a ghost of a smile that made him want to press his mouth to hers.

"Will ye dance with me?" he asked.

She looked to the cleared floor where several couples were already moving in tandem to the lilting music. A thoughtful expression crossed her face as if she were considering refusing his request.

"Please?" he added, recalling Alan's suggestion from the night before.

Lady Isolde returned her attention to him and nodded. "Aye."

Cormac suppressed the jolt of elation at her acceptance and got to his feet, helping her stand as well. Pip leapt up to join them.

"Go on and find Alan," Cormac commanded.

The dog's ears lifted at Alan's name and he immediately trotted off, licking his chops, his full belly round beneath golden fur.

Cormac led Lady Isolde to the dance floor as the tune he

knew drew to a close, and another song began. One whose steps he was unfamiliar with.

Anxiety knotted in his stomach. He could not withdraw his request to dance with her, not after finally having her accept. There would be nothing for it but to manage through the steps and hope he didn't make himself appear a total fool.

6

Isolde stood across from Cormac in preparation for the dance. She could have declined his offer, and he would no doubt have left her to pursue her own endeavors. She could have been free to return to her room where she didn't have to fear being disturbed by Brodie or any other potential suitor.

But there had been something in the softening of his green eyes when he asked her to dance, and how his dimple had appeared when he added "please." The wine she'd consumed had left a delightful heat thrumming in her veins, and she'd been so drawn to him at that moment, she hadn't been able to decline.

She curtseyed as the dance began, and he belatedly offered a bow a second behind the other men. She stepped toward him as the dance dictated, and he rushed to meet her in the middle, his hand thrusting in a rushed motion toward hers. His palm was nearly twice the size of hers and hot against the light touch of her fingertips.

"You don't know the steps, do you?" She asked in a teasing tone.

He gave her a sheepish smile, an endearing expression on such an imposing and confident man. "No' to this dance."

She spoke in a low whisper meant only for him. "We're going to do a turn and then go back to the places where we started. Then we will do it all over again."

He shot her a grateful smile and followed her instructions.

"Why is it you wished to speak to my brother?" She kept her fingers locked in his strong grasp while they moved around one another in a slow circle.

"I want to know why he would let a man like Brodie be promised to ye in the first place." Sutherland stepped back to the original position.

Isolde mouthed the word "bow" as she curtsied to him. He complied. They straightened and came together once more. There was a pleasantly masculine scent about him, the light spice of sandalwood and the underlying smell of leather. "Do you have a sister, Sutherland?"

"Nay. I have only a twin brother."

"Then I think you don't understand how a sister can be such a powerful bargaining tool." She tried to keep the bitterness from her tone.

Sutherland was quiet for a moment as they circled one another again.

"Pause a moment after this so the couple beside us may turn on the next round," she whispered.

He nodded, and they returned to their original places once more. After the couple beside them had completed their slow circle, Isolde and Sutherland came together once more.

His gaze fell upon her with thoughtful consideration. "I think if I had a sister, I would consider her more than chattel to be traded to the highest bidder."

Isolde lifted her brows and did not bother to give voice to her skepticism. She appreciated his noble words, even as she took them with a note of disbelief.

"It appears yer brother has had a change of heart in yer union and issued a challenge to Brodie." The lingering of Sutherland's eyes on her told her he wished to know more.

She waited for him to ask, but he did not.

As they separated in the dance, she realized she had forgotten to give him the instructions for the next dance steps. He bowed to her when he should have remained in place. His mistake was easily noted and caused the other dancers to look in his direction.

He maintained a stoic air, but once everyone's attention fell away, he grimaced with apparent discomfort.

"You don't like to dance, do you?" she asked.

He smirked. "Is it so obvious?"

She shrugged, not wishing to be cruel. "Why did you ask me if you don't care for dancing?"

"I was enjoying my time with ye," he offered in the same shy manner as he'd spoken with earlier when he asked her to dance. "I wasna ready to walk away from ye."

Isolde's cheeks went hot. "Even though my honor is in question?"

The steps separated them at that moment, and she turned her attention away from him rather than witness what expression might be on his face. Mayhap it was scorn or pity or disgust or curiosity. Her stomach clenched with unease. She should not have spoken.

When they came together again, he gently touched her underneath the chin and forced her to look up at him. Concern. It was concern shadowing his eyes. "Did Brodie harm ye?"

"Not in the way you think." Isolde lifted her face from Sutherland's touch with defiance. "He made it look as though he had defiled me. And being a woman, all it takes is a rumor or a staged image to ruin her reputation. My account was not believed, and I was betrothed to a man who had set out to trick my brother into allowing him to have my hand in marriage."

That wasn't the whole of it, of course. Anger burned through her anew. He'd said it had been Gilbert's idea. But why? And

Gilbert had gotten something from their deal as well. What had it been?

"The path of a woman isna an easy one," Sutherland said softly as they stepped apart. "I'd like to help."

The final notes of the melody drew to a close, and the couples around them dispersed. Sutherland approached her and offered her his arm, as noble as any English knight.

Skepticism prodded Isolde's mind as she accepted his gallant gesture. "How do you intend to help?" Was this where he would offer to marry her? A magnanimous proposal to save her? One that would make him a wealthy man?

"I'd like to fight Brodie in Lord Easton's stead," he said.

She frowned. "Do you think my brother incapable of defending my honor?"

He shook his head as though in self-chastisement and cleared his throat. "It isna that I think yer brother incapable. 'Tis only that I feel I am a stronger fighter. I want to ensure ye remain safe."

This was most likely when he would suggest marriage to her in exchange for his aid.

Only the request did not arise. He led her to the Great Hall's exit, as though he knew she wished for nothing more than to return to her rooms.

Matilda caught sight of them from across the room and began the long walk toward them.

"'Tis kind of you to offer," Isolde said.

"Ye shouldna be forced into marriage to someone ye dinna want." His square jaw flexed, and he studied her face for a long moment.

Their proximity was so close that her skin tingled with the heat coming off his body. She couldn't help but observe him as he did her, noting the seriousness of his handsome face and how powerfully strong his chest was. She recalled how she had longed to rest against him earlier that day when he'd saved her and was once more struck with a pang of longing.

"Will ye ask yer brother if I may defend yer honor tomorrow?" There was an intimate silkiness to his brogue that sent a delightful ripple over her skin.

"He's stubborn," she cautioned. "And will do well enough on his own."

Sutherland's lips pressed against one another in a manner that suggested he did not wish to share what was in his thoughts.

"What is it?" She pressed.

"'Tis Lord Easton," he answered with great hesitation. "I fear he may not be strong enough to defeat Brodie."

The pleasant prickle on her skin chilled with fear. She tried to shrug it off as she thanked him for his concern and departed the Great Hall with Matilda. But even as she tried to push away his warning, it seeped into her thoughts and turned them dark with apprehension.

The following day might bring her freedom, aye. But for the first time, she was forced to acknowledge the realization that the battle might also bring her death.

CORMAC WAS RATHER PROUD OF HIMSELF. HE WAS NO SMOOTH-talking courtier like Graham, but he'd done quite well with Isolde that evening. Up to the point where he mentioned the possibility of her brother's death, that is.

He groaned aloud, a sound that was swallowed up by the music and raucous noise around him. He was a damn fool.

He didn't need to be a courtier to know his warning was the least romantic thing he could have possibly said. And yet it was true. Lord Easton was a trained fighter with considerable skill and an enviable dexterity. His strength, however, was lacking. Especially against such an opponent as Brodie.

Prior to Cormac's blunder, the dance had been more pleasant than he'd anticipated. Even with his missteps and ignorance of the moves. He had relished Isolde's smiles and how she had kindly informed him of what moves to prepare for. Her eyes sparkled at him when she danced, reminding him of the sun when it glittered off the sea.

More than anything, however, it was the nearness of her that had given him the most enjoyment.

She wore a delicate rose scent that made him want to bring her closer and breathe her in while stroking a caress down the smoothness of her skin. Her hands had been soft against his. The rest of her would be too. If he ran a finger down her cheek, he knew she would feel like a sun-warmed rose petal. She'd worn her auburn hair back in a braid with a gold circlet fastened around her head.

Movement out of the corner of Cormac's eye caught his attention. Alan. He stood at the opposite end of the long aisle with Pip sitting obediently at his side. Alan waved again, and a flicker of irritation tightened over Cormac at being summoned.

However, Alan's insistence most likely meant he had discovered information about Brodie Ross. Information Cormac was eager to learn.

He took one last glance down the hallway where Isolde and her maid were departing the feast before he quit the Great Hall, exiting into the cool night. He scanned the area for his self-appointed mercenary, finding Alan tucked in a quiet, dark corner.

Cormac joined him in the shadows.

"You were right about the Ross clan." Alan glanced around to ensure no one was listening. "They're up to something."

The news did not surprise Cormac. There had been a twinge of knowing in his gut the moment he'd discovered Brodie and his brothers were to attend an English tournament. "Does it have anything to do with Lady Isolde?"

Alan shook his head. "Not that I'm aware of."

Relief eased some of Cormac's tension. He had hoped she wouldn't be involved, especially considering her contract to wed Brodie Ross. But then, her brother would not call out Brodie over Lady Isolde's honor if he were actively involved.

While the nobles were inside with their cultured music and refined entertainment, the servants were enjoying their freedom outside. No tables needed to be moved in the open space for a dance floor, not when the grass around served the purpose well enough. A man on a mandolin, accompanied by two others on a pipe and a drum, rivaled the music within the castle with a jig that got everyone moving.

There were no fine steps for this dance, but a wild stamping of feet and moving of bodies in time with the thrum of the beat. It was all a great distraction from where Cormac and Alan spoke in the clandestine corner.

"Do ye know the details of their involvement?" Cormac asked.

Alan's mouth tightened at the corners. "It has to do with Prince John."

There had been talk of a plan to put the prince on the throne. It was a risky, foolish venture that would most likely cost many their lives for their parts in such treason.

Cormac lowered his voice. "Do ye think they're part of the coup to overthrow King Richard?"

Alan nodded in response. "Aye, I overheard one of their servants speaking to another noble's squire about the impossibility of one hundred and fifty thousand marks being raised to ensure his release."

King Richard, the true king of England, had been taken captive by the Holy Roman Emperor as he returned home from the last Crusade. Already John had tried to claim that his brother had died on the journey, a lie told in an attempt to claim the throne.

The Scottish were notorious for having a tumultuous relationship with the English. While John had the backing of France, a country whose loyalty had recently extended to Scotland, it didn't surprise Cormac one bit that the Rosses would stoop to such a level as to overthrow a king for their own benefit.

"I'm sure comments on the attempt to raise funds for the ransom warranted a few grumbles." Cormac snorted.

Alan rolled his eyes in agreement. Nobles were feeling the emptiness in their own purses in light of Eleanor of Aquitaine's attempt to scrape together the funds to recover her son, King Richard.

"Was there anything else?" Cormac asked.

Pip leaned heavily against Alan's leg, resulting in the mercenary stretching a hand down to pat his dog. "Nothing for now."

There would be more, of course. They both knew it. Treachery often ran deep and had more tunnels than a termite's nest.

"Ye did a fine job, Alan." Cormac nodded his appreciation toward his new mercenary.

Alan's face lit up, and his skinny chest puffed out. "I'm glad to have pleased you, sir. Is there anything I can do for you?"

Cormac folded his arms over his chest and watched the crowd dancing wildly to an English tune he was unfamiliar with. "Inform Duncan and Lachlan of what ye've told me and keep an eye on the Ross clan, especially Brodie. And if ye hear from my brother, ensure he knows as well, aye?"

Alan's jaw set with determination, and even Pip straightened to attention at his master's side. "I won't let you down, sir."

Something about Lady Isolde being promised to Brodie still churned in Cormac's gut. Aye, her brother was defending her honor now, but why?

Cormac recalled the scene where Lord Easton had challenged Brodie, the way the English lord had clenched his slender hand into a fist after having removed his gauntlet. The action stuck in Cormac's mind for some reason, and a note of unease nipped at the back of his mind.

There was something amiss.

While he didn't know what it was exactly, he vowed to arrive on the practice field the following morning in time to watch the battle for Lady Isolde's honor. While there, he would try to convince the earl to allow him to fight instead.

That failing, he wanted to be there to ensure the Englishman didn't get killed. And if he did, at least someone could be there to protect Lady Isolde. Regardless of how the events transpired the following day, Cormac knew blood would be shed. He only hoped that not too much of it belonged to the Earl of Easton.

❦ 7 ❧

Isolde's trepidation about her upcoming battle with Brodie did not diminish through the night. In fact, it increased from a tumble of thoughts to a tumultuous storm of worry.

She was awake long before the gentle creaks and murmurs of the servants moving about began. Her stomach roiled with unease, and her head ached with the discomfort of a sleepless night.

Matilda drew open the bed curtain and peeked in at her. "My lady, 'tis time."

Isolde removed herself from the bed and allowed Matilda to gently wash her face and comb her hair before preparing her for the fight. It did not escape Isolde's notice that Matilda's brows were drawn together as though she were in physical pain.

"Are you certain you must do this, my lady?" Tears shone in the maid's eyes.

Isolde notched her chin upward with determination. "I am certain I have no other choice and that I have been well-trained for this moment." Mayhap her bravado in front of Matilda might pass off onto her own awareness.

Isolde could use all the confidence she could muster.

Matilda did not protest Isolde's decision again as she dressed her mistress in Gilbert's armor. Though the padding beneath the chainmail had been set in cedarwood to help remove the rank of stale sweat, the mustiness still rose over the metallic odor of chainmail. And beneath it all was the coppery tinge of her own fear.

She settled the helm into place and gave herself a moment to adjust to the limited visibility while Matilda belted the sword to her side.

At last, Isolde was prepared for battle.

Upon arrival to the practice field, any concerns she might have harbored over being unable to locate Brodie dissolved. He had arrived before her and waited impatiently for her to show. He was not the only one. A small band of men gathered around the area in anticipation. Among them were Sutherland and the slender mercenary who had come to their aid after the joust the prior day.

Pip caught sight of her and ran at her with such speed that it pulled his pink tongue from the corner of his mouth. His broad front paws hefted into the air and landed on her thighs, practically knocking her to the ground with the impact. Wouldn't that look fine? To be felled by a mid-sized dog before Brodie could even land a single blow.

She scratched the spot behind his ears and whispered a command for him to return to Alan, one she'd heard Cormac say often. The hound did as he was bade, but with great hesitation and apparent regret.

Sutherland caught sight of her and met her halfway. "Let me fight in yer stead, my lord."

"Nay, Sutherland," Isolde said brusquely in Gilbert's petulant tone. "This is my man to take down and so help me God, I shall do it with my own blade."

"He's far stronger than ye." Sutherland's voice took on a warning tone that slithered a trail of ice down Isolde's spine.

"He's nothing I cannot handle," she replied. "What concern is it of yours?"

"I've come to know yer sister," Sutherland said in a low voice. "She's a good woman who has been taken advantage of. A fact that doesna sit well with me."

"Nor I," Isolde replied. "And so, I shall address this now, as the man I am."

Sutherland put his hand to Isolde's chest to stop her. It was all she could do to keep from drawing back as though she'd been struck. Her breasts were strapped down, aye, but would he feel the swells of her bound bosom through the layers of batting and chain and linen? Tingles raced over the area he'd touched, intimate despite her inability to feel anything more than the slight pressure of his hand.

"Ye're far more dexterous than Brodie," Sutherland said, oblivious to the reaction coursing through her like fire. "He'll be moving slow given his size. Use that to yer advantage."

Isolde nodded her thanks and brushed past him to the center of a small circle of men where Brodie awaited her. The Highlander snarled at her in greeting and did not even wait for her to prepare before plunking his helm upon his head and charging. She dodged the first blow of his sword, but was not so lucky with the punch that followed.

His metal fist slammed into her side with the force of a hammer. The breath gusted from her lungs, and she nearly collapsed. The only thing keeping her upright after such a strike was the very real possibility she might never get up if she fell.

She swung her sword, but it glanced off his shoulder. No doubt, the scant power behind her own weapon was not nearly as impactful as his. He roared his irritation at the blow. The back of his hand crashed into her helm, knocking it sideways and sending her whole world plunging into darkness, with a shrill ringing in her ears.

Her breath panted in great heaving gasps.

Your helm.

She calmed her frenzied thoughts and righted her helmet. Once more, Brodie came into view. He lumbered toward her and drove his sword down with two hands. She managed to evade the blow. The grass where she'd been split against the sharp weight of his blade, revealing a wound in the dark soil beneath.

While he was still hefting his weapon to reclaim it from the earth, Isolde fell back on the advice Sutherland had so generously imparted. She was dexterous. Faster than most men. She rushed behind Brodie, curled a leg around his feet, and shoved with all her strength. He pitched backward like a falling tree, arms flailing.

Isolde wasted no time—she climbed atop him and shoved off his helm. Before she could settle her blade to his throat, he withdrew a rod from the belt at his waist and whipped it at her wrist.

Pain exploded into a thousand white-hot stars before her eyes. This time, she did freeze, made immobile by the brilliance of the agony. Brodie grabbed her and flipped her onto her back. Her helm rocked back against the ground, rattling in her ears.

The slit of her vision faced up to a cloudy gray sky, rendering her blind to her opponent. His weight pushed down on her like a crushing millstone. She gasped, but her chest struggled to fill with air against the press of his body. Her right hand buzzed with pain and clenched around nothing.

She had lost her sword.

The helm tilted as though being pried from her face.

She would be found out.

A rush of energy surged through her, exploding with a power of which she had not thought herself capable. Nearly blind from her limited visibility, she arched her hips up, throwing him off her. In a single move, she leapt atop him, whipped out her dagger with her left hand and held it to his throat.

"Concede," she gasped in whatever imitation of Gilbert's voice she could muster from her rasping throat.

"Aye," Brodie snarled. "I concede."

She pushed off of him and strumbled backward. Only then did she adjust her helm to bring the narrow line of her vision correctly over her eyes. Brodie lumbered to his feet, his face dark with rage.

She had won.

The realization dawned on her like a beam of sunshine.

She had won.

Her freedom.

Her honor.

She—a woman, valued as little more than chattel to those who would trade her like property—had defeated a Scottish warrior. When no man would stand up for her, she had defended her own honor.

And she had won.

Brodie stalked toward her, his breath coming out in growling huffs. "Ye dinna win that easily, my lord." He said the last two words with a sneer of condemnation.

He ripped the gauntlet off one hairy hand and threw it at her feet. She bent over to see it through her helm. There it lay, glittering metal in the muted sunlight against the battered grass. A counterchallenge.

A ball of frustration tightened in her throat.

Tears welled in her eyes beneath the protective barrier of her helm.

Nay. It was too unfair. She had won. *She had won.*

She swallowed, incapable of summoning any kind of reply.

"This time, I'm challenging yer honor and yer inability to comply with our arrangement," Brodie said in a low, menacing tone. "But I willna fight ye myself. Prepare to battle my da's best champion."

Isolde didn't know who his champion was, but she knew well that tone. She'd heard it before when he'd pinned her against the wall and pushed up her skirts. She'd heard it again outside the stands at the start of the joust. And now it sent a shiver of panic skittering down her spine.

"Yer sister will be mine, ye shite." Brodie shoved past her, leaving his gauntlet behind, lying lifeless in the grass like an omen.

Her body was battered from the battle, but it hadn't mattered. None of it did.

Brodie would find a way to win. And once more, she was a helpless victim to the ways of men.

⚜

No one in the surrounding band of people moved after Brodie's departure. The battle had been brutal. At one point, Cormac was certain the Earl of Easton had lost.

Judging by the sag of the smaller man's shoulders, he still considered his victory a loss regardless. And indeed, it was.

Pip shifted from one paw to the other, where he stood anxiously between Alan and Cormac.

"What's wrong with yer dog?" Cormac demanded.

Alan frowned down at his pet. "I've never seen him like this."

Lord Easton turned from the practice field toward the castle, his back straight despite cradling his arm.

Pip whimpered and strode forward several steps.

"Pip, stay," Alan demanded.

The dog didn't listen. He broke into a run toward Lord Easton and nudged the earl's leg with his nose. His sharp whines carried on the breeze back toward them.

Alan cast a confused glance at Cormac. "I don't understand..."

But Cormac did. The only time Pip reacted with such excitement to anyone other than Alan was with Lady Isolde. Regarding the fair lady herself, it had not escaped Cormac's notice that she had not been in attendance for Lord Easton's fight.

If one's brother would stand against a great foe in defense of his sister's honor, it was a great disservice for her not to have even shown to display her support.

"Did ye ever notice Lady Isolde and the Earl of Easton are never in the same location at the same time?" Cormac muttered to Alan.

The mercenary's forehead puckered, and his jaw unhinged with shock. "You're right." He shook his head. "But it can't be. Either Lord Easton is a lovely man with a pair of very convincing duckies." He turned his gaze to where Lord Easton slowly strode away with Pip following at his side. "Or Lady Isolde—" He shook his head harder with obvious disbelief. "It can't be, sir. Ladies don't fight. Especially not like that. I thought Lord Easton was going to tear Brodie's head from his body."

Cormac ran his hands over the edge of his jaw, scrubbing the prickling whiskers. Alan was correct. It was highly unlikely. And yet...

He strode off after the earl. "Ye fought well, my lord."

"Not well enough." There was a tremble to the arrogant tone.

Was the voice feminine beneath the air of pretension?

"I can fight for ye." It was foolish of Cormac to offer, but he couldn't help himself. Especially if Lord Easton truly was Lady Isolde.

Everyone knew Brodie's champion, Edmund the Braw, was a beast of a man. Cormac could very well die.

Lord Easton most assuredly would.

A sniffle came from inside Lord Easton's helm. Cormac found it strange that the man wore it even out of combat. Come to think of it, Cormac had never seen the earl's face, and his suspicions re-emerged with force.

Lord Easton slowed. "'Tis a generous offer, Sutherland, but I fear this is a battle I must fight. I would gladly accept your council, however, should you be kind enough to offer it."

"Aye, I'll do anything I can to help." Cormac considered the smaller man and wondered again if it was Lady Isolde's slender body encased in chainmail and padding. If so, had she bound her breasts beneath?

He recalled how they'd been full and firm in her gown at the feast.

He also realized he was staring at the earl's chest in an attempt to make out any swells of feminine flesh. His cheeks heated, and he snapped his fingers at the dog. "Pip, leave the earl be."

Pip's tail dipped between his legs, and he issued another soft whine before trotting off to return to Alan.

"If you'll excuse me," the earl muttered.

"Of course." Cormac stopped abruptly to give the earl his space and watched as the Englishman slowly walked away with a decidedly unfeminine gait.

As the day went on, Cormac searched for Lady Isolde as well as Lord Easton. Despite his efforts and those of his men, neither were to be found.

That evening at the feast, Cormac half-expected Lady Isolde to have taken her meal in her rooms and was surprised to find her sitting in her usual spot at the high table. This time, she wore a silk kirtle as pale blue as her eyes with her auburn hair coiled into a silver caul. Candlelight cast golden shadows over her creamy skin and teased at the hollows of her collarbones and throat.

However, Lady Isolde was not the only person to catch his notice.

Brodie wove through the stream of people, his focus set on her. Cormac was closer and quickened his pace to ensure he arrived before his rival. In the end, it was Pip who beat them all and immediately fell to his place at her feet.

"May I join ye, Lady Isolde?" Cormac asked.

She glanced up at him and nodded, "Aye."

"I hope yer brother fares well after the fight this morn," Cormac offered.

Lady Isolde nodded but did not say anything. A pained expression touched her eyes, and she swallowed hard.

"And how do ye fare?" He asked.

She cast her eyes demurely to her lap. "I am quite well. Thank you."

"My lady," Cormac lowered his voice to speak privately to her. "Please know you can speak to me with honesty."

She lifted her head, meeting his gaze, and sighed heavily. "If I'm being entirely honest, I'm vexed."

"I imagine most would be in yer position." Cormac cut a slice of meat from the shank of venison laid before them and placed it on Isolde's pewter plate.

She pressed her lips together.

He'd said the wrong thing again. Irritation for his own blundering tightened along his back.

"I have to wonder if you are where you want to be." She lifted her head and gave him a brazen stare.

"Do ye think I'm no'?" he asked.

"I saw you earlier before the feast began." Color blossomed in her cheeks and she slid her gaze from his, but not before he caught the brilliance of hurt in the pale blue depths.

"I only just arrived," he replied.

She nodded, evidently not believing him, and nudged the venison on her plate with her eating dagger.

Her behavior was...odd.

"I wasn't aware you were acquainted with Lady Clara," she said abruptly.

Lady Clara? Cormac searched his mind for the name when understanding dawned on him. "I think I understand now."

She sank the point of her eating dagger into the meat, so it stood upright and looked at him.

"My brother, Graham," Cormac explained. "My *twin* brother, Graham. He holds an affinity for the lass."

"Your twin?" she repeated slowly.

He nodded. "I'm older, which is why I'm chieftain. But we look the same. We drove our mum nearly mad when we were boys as we were always switching our names to confuse her." He chuckled at the memory.

All at once, the tension relaxed somewhat from her shoulders, and a tight smile touched her lips. "Forgive me, I..." She shook her head. "It doesn't matter."

Cormac's own stress eased somewhat. If she'd seen Graham and Lady Clara and had assumed Graham was Cormac, did her reaction mean she was jealous?

He practically grinned at the thought. "I apologize if ye mixed us up," Cormac replied. "It wouldna be the first time. I thought ye were upset over the counter-challenge."

Her expression hardened, and she took a sip of wine from a goblet that appeared nearly empty. "Have you heard of Brodie's champion?"

Cormac filled his own plate and reached for a roll. It had long since gone cold and would probably be hard as a stone by now. Tournaments often had such problems with their food. Too many people to serve, and too much food left out to cool while waiting to be delivered to the proper table. At least the meat was hot.

He put a bite in his mouth and chewed the tender morsel slowly as he considered how to answer Isolde's question. Edmund the Braw was a man whose head rose over all others and whose arms were thick as tree trunks. Defeating him would be difficult for any warrior, even Cormac. But especially for the Earl of Easton.

Especially for a lady if Lady Isolde was indeed masquerading as a man. Cormac regarded her, and his chest drew tight.

"He is powerful," Cormac said eventually.

"I see." Lady Isolde's lips pinched into a narrow line. She reached for some bread, and the draped blue silk sleeve of her gown caught at the table's edge and drew back over her wrist to reveal her forearm. A vivid, purple-black bruise showed like ink on her fair skin.

She quickly covered it, and Cormac pretended to have been too fixed on his meal to have noticed.

But he had seen it.

And now he knew with certainty.

The Earl of Easton had not defeated Brodie that morn. The victor had been Lady Isolde. Which meant it was she who would go up against Edmund the Braw. And she who would die.

Unless Cormac could convince her to let him fight in her stead.

8

Isolde should not have attended the feast. Her body ached with every breath, and her chest throbbed with every blazing beat of her heart.

However, she needed to maintain appearances. It would not do to have her miss a feast simply because Gilbert had been counter-challenged after his win. Or at least, that was what she told herself.

She knew the truth. And judging by the little smile Matilda had given as she brushed Isolde's hair to a brilliant shine, she knew it too.

The truth had everything to do with the man sitting at Isolde's side. Sutherland.

That truth had been confirmed in the stab of jealousy she'd experienced when she'd thought she'd seen him with Lady Clara. In hindsight, she realized it couldn't have been Sutherland. Not when the other man had such a cocky smile, and his gait had been more relaxed as he walked alongside Lady Clara.

Sutherland was far too rigid. Stoic.

She tugged down the sleeve of her dress, ensuring it covered her bruise. A quick glance confirmed he had not seen it on her arm. Thanks be to God. The last thing she needed in this complicated mess of events was for him to know she was playing the part of her brother as well as herself.

The serving girl refilled Isolde's goblet with more wine. Already the numbing effects of the beverage heated through Isolde's blood and eased the throb from the worst of her injuries.

She lifted the full chalice to her lips and drank deeply before addressing Sutherland. "How do you think my brother will fare against a man like Edmund the Braw?" She kept her attention fixed on Sutherland to gauge his reaction.

His jaw tensed, and his gaze flicked briefly away. Not a good sign. He shifted in his seat. "I must be honest with ye, my lady. Edmund the Braw is one of the largest men in Scotland. He's verra powerful and skilled."

The muscles along her back knotted at his wary tone. She gave a terse nod for him to continue.

"I believe if yer brother were to fight Edmund, he wouldna fare well." Sutherland watched her carefully as he spoke.

She looked into his green eyes, drawing strength from the impenetrable man before her. It was one of the reasons she'd longed to see him. His confidence and the power he carried with such ease. She had need of it, of him.

She was struck once more with the desire to ease against his hard body, to lay her head to his chest and let his arms curl around her in an embrace. Had she ever had such protective comfort?

Not from her brother, nor their father. From her mother, aye. But her mother's arms, though tender, had been frail and delicate. And there had been love, so much love that it caused an ache to form at the back of her throat.

Isolde wanted love of a different form now, and comfort. But she also wanted someone whose strength she could share. A man like Sutherland.

"I dinna mean to make ye cry." He reached a hand toward her

face as though he meant to brush away a tear and stopped abruptly.

The way he caught himself reminded her where they were: in the middle of a feast, surrounded by courtiers, with Brodie hovering somewhere in the near distance. Such stark realizations made her want to cry more. The entire effort of her ruse, the fight she had endured, the risk she had taken—all of it had been futile.

She hastily swiped the tear from her cheek.

"I know ye're close with yer brother," Sutherland said gently.

Isolde almost gave a sardonic bark of laughter. He had no idea exactly how close she and Gilbert had become at the tournament.

"Do ye think Lord Easton will change his mind and allow me to fight Edmund the Braw in his stead?" Sutherland asked.

She recalled Sutherland's offer—one she'd declined out of bravado. Now though, she took his suggestion with more consideration.

She had barely survived her victory with Brodie and hadn't emerged unscathed. Sutherland was not a man for dramatic statements. He had sparred with her, and if he deemed her skills against Edmund the Braw would be inadequate, she knew he spoke in earnest.

If there was a possibility of her mayhap being killed, then there was a possibility that Cormac could die as well. He was the chieftain of a clan who relied on him, and she was simply a woman who had little foothold in the world, save noble birth and wealth.

She could not allow him to die in her stead. Not when it was her honor, and her decisions, which took them down this path.

She shook her head, her mind made up. "He would not allow you to fight in his stead." She folded her hands in her lap and stared hard at her interlaced fingers.

Coming to the feast had been a mistake. Seeing Sutherland again had been a mistake. It had all been indulgent and foolish.

"I canna allow Lord Easton to go into a fight that he canna survive," Sutherland said.

The serving girl approached with a flagon of wine and tipped more of the dark-red liquid into Isolde's goblet. Isolde waited for the woman to leave before replying, "You have people depending on you, Sutherland."

"Does yer brother no' have people relying on him as well?"

He had a point. Isolde lifted the goblet with her left hand to avoid the bruise on her right arm from showing again. She let the rich wine wash down her throat in a burning swallow that roiled in her stomach. After this goblet, she decided, she would have another and mayhap another.

Anything to slow the churn of her mind and warm the creeping chill of fear in her veins.

"Lady Isolde." Sutherland's voice was gentle with his Scottish burr, the tone low and intimate. "I want to help ye."

She finished off her goblet and nudged it toward the edge of the table so the serving wench might see it more readily. She returned her attention to Sutherland, and the protest died on her lips.

His mouth was fuller than she'd noticed before, appearing soft and pink compared to the bristle of his hard, whiskered jaw. She had the sudden urge to kiss him. Her palms tingled, longing for the rasp of that short, wiry hair against them, her lips eager to discover if his mouth truly was as supple as it looked.

A splash sounded as her goblet was filled once more. Bile burned up the back of Isolde's throat, and the room rocked about in a dizzying spin.

"I should go," she murmured.

"The feast is no' yet over." His eyes narrowed with apparent concern. "Are ye well?"

Isolde got to her feet, which only set the world twirling faster. She tipped to the side, but Sutherland caught her. Pain exploded at her injured arm, and she cried out, drawing it protectively to her chest.

"Forgive me, I dinna mean to hurt ye. I merely tried to keep ye upright."

"Is she well?" A woman asked in a snide tone.

"Too much excitement," Sutherland said.

He didn't leave her side. Instead, he put a supportive arm over her shoulders to aid in keeping her upright. She leaned into him, not because she needed to, but because she wanted to. Aye—with every aching beat of her hollow heart, she wanted to. He was solid under her touch, his body heat radiating through his fine tunic. She longed to close her eyes and revel at his strength until she was lulled into sleep in the cradle of his arms.

His essence was all around her, the hint of sandalwood and wonderful masculinity. She inhaled, savoring his scent. Her exhale came out in a contented hum.

"You have no idea how much I've longed for this," she whispered.

Or did she whisper it? Mayhap it had merely been a thought.

It didn't matter. Nothing mattered because she might soon die. Or be forced to wed Brodie Ross. Either future was dismal.

"What ails her?" Matilda's voice pitched with concern.

"Wine," Sutherland replied quietly.

"I'll see to her," Matilda said.

"I can help her to her rooms," Sutherland said.

Matilda hesitated. "Aye, very well. I don't think I'd be strong enough to get her above stairs."

Velvety darkness winked in and out of Isolde's world. She felt herself lifted as if she were floating and carried through a cold hallway before being delivered into a warm chamber and pillowy bed that seemed to embrace her whole body.

The click of a door startled Isolde from her dreamless slumber.

"My lady." Matilda settled beside the bed and filled Isolde's vision. "I've never seen you in such a state. What ails you?"

"Oh, Matilda," Isolde said miserably. Tears ran hot from her eyes and soaked into the pillow as her pent-up emotions finally were free to wash over her. "I think I'm going to die."

۞

CORMAC SCANNED THE SURROUNDING FIELD OF MEN. SOME donned their finest surcoats over their chainmail in preparation for the joust. He wore an old tunic over his chainmail, eager more for practice rather than the daily jousts.

"I signed you up for the melee." Alan smiled so wide that all his teeth showed.

Cormac lifted a brow. "Why would ye do that?"

The sky rumbled overhead as flecks of rain began to spit at them.

Alan framed his hand over his face like a visor. "Now you have an excuse to remain here through the end of the tournament." He lifted his brows up and down as if they were in on a secret plot together.

"I said I was part of the melee to appease Lady Isolde," Cormac replied. "I dinna have actually to join it."

Alan opened his mouth, paused, then closed it and dropped his head. Guilt tightened in Cormac's chest. He put a hand to the mercenary's shoulder and gave him a reassuring squeeze. At that very moment, Pip's ears perked up, his attention pinpointing on a lone man in armor who wore his helm, even in the rain.

Lord Easton.

Or, most likely, Lady Isolde.

The dog panted excitedly, leapt to his feet and dashed over to Lord Easton.

For now, Cormac did not question his suspicion. Especially

not after he had accidentally grabbed her injured arm in his attempt to keep her from falling the prior eve.

He could still recall how her body had rested so easily against his, the sweet scent of roses tempting him to tilt her head upwards to have better access to her mouth. He hadn't, of course. But it didn't mean he hadn't been tempted.

Especially when she'd inhaled deeply, as though smelling him and breathed out those words that had haunted him through the night.

"You have no idea how much I've longed for this."

Had she truly longed for him the way he'd longed for her? Most likely, the wine had put such words in her mouth. She had consumed a hearty amount. But he could not quell his hopeful thoughts.

The rain came down in earnest as she approached in her brother's armor.

Cormac clasped her forearm as he would do with any other warrior. "Good morrow, Lord Easton. I see ye've joined us on this bonny summer day."

"I couldn't let you Scots enjoy all the fun," Isolde said.

She did a fine job of masking her voice to sound like a whiny earl. Now that he knew her secret, however, he could detect the underlying femininity. How had he missed it before?

"I spoke with yer sister last night," Cormac said. "I trust she is well?"

Isolde scoffed. "Foolish chit doesn't know her own limitation when it comes to wine."

Cormac had to fight to keep from chuckling at her own self-rebuke. "Did she tell ye what I said to her?"

"She did not rouse as I was breaking my fast this morn. I dare say we will not be seeing her for the remainder of the day."

Lightning streaked overhead, and a roll of thunder snarled. Fat drops of rain hammered down at them.

Cormac widened his stance. "I'd like ye to reconsider my offer to stand in yer stead with Edmund the Braw."

"My reply is still nay." Though Cormac couldn't see inside the helm, he was certain Isolde was shaking her head within.

"He's a powerful warrior," Cormac cautioned. "The best Scotland has ever known."

Isolde was quiet, and the pinging of raindrops pelting her helm filled the silence. "As I said before, help me by training me to beat him."

Cormac clenched his teeth. Instruction would still not be enough to save Isolde. However, if he could train with her and show her where she lacked strength, mayhap she might change her mind and allow him to fight Edmund the Braw.

"Aye." Cormac led Isolde to an awning-covered overhang to provide some reprieve from the worst of the rain. "I'll help ye, but I'd like a favor in return."

Pip huddled against Isolde's leg, eyeing the storm as though it meant him harm. "Of course you do," Isolde replied in a haughty tone, unlike her usual appealing demeanor.

Again, Cormac bit back a chuckle. For all her sweetness and consideration, she played the part of an entitled noble well.

"I'd like to get advice from ye on how to speak to Lady Isolde." Somehow, he managed to proffer his request with a straight face.

Another grumble of thunder came from the blackened clouds.

"Why ever would you care for advice on how to speak to her?" Isolde asked sharply.

"Because I've no' ever been good at speaking with women." Cormac shrugged, trying to appear nonchalant. "I've no' ever been interested in trying to appeal to a lass, before her. Which only makes me say foolish things even more when I'm around her. I wondered if ye might offer some suggestions. Assuming ye know what she likes to speak about."

The shush of the falling rain filled the silence. "Aye," she replied finally. "She wants respect and to be seen as more than a prize to wed. For someone to appreciate the person that she is beneath her beauty and wealth."

The patter of rain began to slow to a steady drizzle.

Cormac nodded. He could do that.

"I'll give you more than that later, after I've thought on it some," Isolde replied. "The rain is slowing, and we haven't a second to waste."

He followed onto the muddy grass. Pip, however, remained under the awning and was joined by Alan.

"When ye go to strike, draw the blade up with the strength in yer belly rather than yer arms." Cormac clasped his weapon's hilt in his hands and swung it toward a wooden post with just the strength of his arms. He repeated the action again, this time drawing the strength from his stomach. The pole split in half.

Isolde approached and did as he had done. On her second strike, the top of the pole went flying and splashed into a puddle several paces away.

"Did ye feel the difference?" He asked.

"Aye," she replied. "Show me more."

And he did. They spent the better of the morning going over various battle techniques. The lightened rain did not hold and eventually became a downpour that drenched them, weighing down the gambeson beneath their chainmail as well as their surcoats. Other men practiced alongside them, paying them little mind.

Cormac showed Isolde how to throw a man over her back despite her size and bade her try it herself. Unfortunately, when she grabbed him suddenly and slung him over her shoulder, her helm slipped from her head and plopped into the sodden ground alongside where Cormac lay face-up in a puddle of mud.

She froze where she stood, exposed to anyone who could see her face. Granted, the padded hood of her armor covered her long auburn hair, but her features were decidedly feminine.

Far too much to pass for a man.

Her mouth fell open, and her wide blue gaze darted about. Quick as the lightning still forking through the sky above them, Cormac grabbed her helm, settled it on her head and dragged her from the practice field. He didn't know where he intended to take her until they were already in his tent with the flap drawn firmly closed.

Rain pattered over the thick, waxed linen of the tent, but other than those sounds, the tent was heavy with palpable silence.

"Lady Isolde?" he asked softly.

She pulled in a breath and lifted the helm from her head, revealing her beautiful face with bits of her fiery hair slicked against her skin beneath her padded hood. "Aye," she replied. "'Tis me."

9

Isolde stood before Sutherland, shamefaced and exposed. He knew her secret.

She waited for his scorn. Mayhap his disgust.

Instead, he stared at her with incredulity. "Who taught ye how to fight?"

"Hugh," she answered readily in her surprise at his response. "Our Master of the Guard."

"Are ye all right?" He asked the question with such tenderness that it edged into the most fragile part of her heart and made an ache of emotion tighten at the back of her throat.

"Aye, I'm fine," she answered tentatively.

"I mean from the beating ye took yesterday." He glanced down at her body, worry bright in his eyes. "I've seen warriors who struggle with hits like ye took. I've no' ever imagined a well-born lady might withstand them. Are ye badly hurt?"

"I've had worse." She grinned. It was true. She had.

At the beginning of those early training days with Hugh, there had been cracked ribs and bruises and scrapes. All had been hidden with jewelry and veils and gritted teeth.

Sutherland laughed good-naturedly at her comment. It was

the first time she'd heard him laugh. The sound was warm and pleasant, one she realized she'd like to hear more of. His green eyes crinkled at the corners, and his smile eased the severity of his face, giving him an almost boyish handsomeness.

She looked around the narrow tent. There were two cots within. Mayhap one for his brother who looked just like him. She recalled seeing him before, the man who looked identical to Sutherland, and the flicker of jealousy she'd felt when she'd seen him with Lady Clara.

Aside from the men's cots, there were two bags set on a wax-lined sheet to keep them dry and several surcoats and tunics hanging from a line at the back. No doubt to keep them from wrinkling thoroughly in the bags.

"Ye're serious." His mirth faded into a sincere expression. "I hope ye've no' had many more injuries than what I saw ye endure with Brodie."

"Is it possible to become a warrior without learning to take a hit?" she asked.

A muscle worked in Sutherland's jaw. "Why did ye do it?"

She returned her attention to him. His dark hair hung damp around his face. Even wet and cold, he looked inviting. "Why did I learn to fight?" she clarified.

He opened his hands in a helpless gesture. "Aye. And why did ye fight Brodie?"

Isolde didn't know where to start. There was too much to tell. So many years that had built up to where she was now that she had shared with no one but Matilda. Sutherland seemed to sense her uncertainty and stepped closer, lowering his voice to something gentler and more tender.

"Mayhap, tell me why ye learned to fight." He lifted his shoulder in a partial shrug. "'Tis a rarity to find a noblewoman who knows how to fight like a knight."

There was admiration in his tone, and it pulled the corners of her lips into a smile that memories quickly dissolved.

"I started my training several years ago," Isolde shut her eyes as that night so long ago came rushing back to her. "Our stronghold was attacked. It was before we had the stone keep that we do now, back when our fortifications were made of wood. We were being attacked by a rival lord who wanted our land. My father went to fight, as did my brother and all of their men. My mother was already in heaven then, thanks be to God, for no one thought to protect the women. The maid I had at the time and I were left entirely alone."

She could remember all too well how the time had dragged, weighted with uncertainty and fear while the shouts and cries of battle sounded from beneath her chamber window.

"The men were able to break down the walls easily and forcibly entered the keep. One man hacked through my door with an axe. We waited, Mary and I, terrified with each strike of the axe head into the door. Bit by bit, the door splintered apart. We had not a single dagger between us. Not even a pair of sewing shears." Even to speak of it now made the terror flutter to life like something living and all-consuming within her chest.

"He killed Mary first." Isolde shuddered. "An axe is a terribly gruesome way to die."

Mary's image rose in Isolde's mind, the woman who had cared for her since infancy, lying face down in a pool of her own gore. There had been so much blood. A puddle of it spread beneath the woman, soaking her blue kirtle to a glistening black red.

"He came for me next, with Mary's blood still dripping from the axe." Fright sucked at her lungs, pulling air from them even now. She inhaled, and through the musky scent of sweaty male and the dampness of a rainstorm, she could still detect the odor of blood.

"All I could do was scream." And that was exactly what she'd done. She'd screamed and screamed and screamed until her throat was raw.

"Just as the man was pulling his arm back to strike my skull with his wicked weapon, Hugh rushed in and ran him through before my very eyes." Isolde swallowed down the taste of bile and opened her eyes to stare down at her hands. She still wore her gauntlets, though the gloves beneath were sodden and icy. "I had never witnessed a violent death before that day and was overwhelmed by its horror. I never wanted to be defenseless and at the mercy of my fears again. I bade Hugh promise to teach me to defend myself, to ensure I might never again be in such a helpless position. For had he not heard me crying out that day, I would be dead."

She looked up when Sutherland did not respond and found him watching her with a clenched jaw.

"Ye shouldna have been left alone."

"I'm stronger for what I endured." She lifted her chin. "I needn't worry about being helpless now. Not when I can save myself."

"Ye shouldna have to save yerself," he growled.

She knew his anger was not directed at her. Still, it made her long to soothe him. "I do not regret the strong woman it made me. I only wish it had not happened at the expense of Mary."

He nodded, more to himself than her. "Hugh did a fine job training ye. I imagine it wasna easy to hide from yer father and brother."

She gave a mirthless laugh. "How did you know I had to keep my training a secret?"

"Ye're a well-born lady. It is assumed yer job is to wed and create heirs, aye?"

She studied him to determine if he was mocking her. His expression remained serious. In the distance, a cheer rose, most likely from the jousting stands.

"What do you think?" she asked.

"I think ye shouldna have been in a situation where ye dinna feel protected. I vow to ye at this moment that will never happen to ye again. No' as long as I'm alive."

His words brought a comfort she should not have relished. But she did. They enveloped her with the warmth of his promise and made everything inside her glow.

"Why were ye fighting against Brodie?" Sutherland pressed. "Why did Lord Easton no' do it for ye?"

The embrace of pleasure at the moment cooled. "My brother does not share your sentiment on ensuring ladies under his care are well protected." Isolde didn't bother to keep the bitterness from her reply. "'Twas he who caught me with Brodie. He blamed me, of course. After all, 'tis never the man's fault. The fault always lies with a woman."

"Ye came to defend yer own honor because he was too much of a coward?" Sutherland surmised.

Isolde nodded.

Outside, another round of cheers erupted from the joust.

"What happened with Brodie?" Sutherland asked.

Isolde explained the details she'd kept from him previously, how Brodie had bade her assist him in locating the Great Hall after having sent Matilda on a task to draw her away from Isolde. Once he had her alone in the hall, how he pushed her against the wall and shoved up her skirt to ensure that they were caught in a suggestive position.

"He didn't touch me." Isolde didn't know why she felt she had to offer that reassurance to Sutherland. "But he might as well have, for the opinion of all the men who saw."

Sutherland's face darkened to an alarming shade of red. "I truly regret that ye dinna allow me to battle him that day on yer behalf."

Isolde regarded Sutherland warily. "Why do you say that?"

"Because it would have been the best opportunity for me to kill him."

CORMAC WAS ENTIRELY SINCERE ABOUT WANTING TO KILL Brodie. The hurt and embarrassment blazing in Isolde's face and the tears shining in her eyes made him want to slay someone. Brodie would be a good start. Then her brother would do nicely as a second.

Cormac couldn't stop recalling how hard Brodie had struck her. How even *Cormac himself* had hit her through the course of their practice when he thought she was her brother.

He tugged off his gauntlets and let them fall unceremoniously onto his pack on the floor. "Let me see yer arm."

She didn't move to slide off her gauntlet or lift up her sleeve. He closed the distance between them with a single step and carefully eased back the padded coif and chainmail hood from her head. All of her hair was visible now; the limp auburn waves plastered to her face and scalp with a braid that ran down the back of her gambeson and chainmail. She watched him with wide blue eyes as he did this, saying nothing.

But not stopping him either.

"Please," he said in a quiet voice.

He longed to caress her cheek, to warm her cold, damp skin with his hands. Instead, he lifted her arm and gently pulled off her gauntlet, the leather of her glove beneath cold and swollen with rainwater. Her fingers were slender and fine; her nails perfectly rounded and clean. Lady's hands.

Color touched her cheeks. "Hugh always insisted I wore gloves when we practiced so my palms wouldn't become callused."

"Smart man." Cormac pushed up the sleeve of her chainmail and the gambeson beneath, exposing the entirety of the bruise. It was as long as the hilt of his blade and a dark purple black.

He ran his finger over her injury, his touch light as a feather. Her skin blazed under his fingertips.

Concern and anger twisted into an ugly knot in his gut. "Are ye sure 'tis no' broken?"

She bit her lip and shook her head. "I've had a break before. I know what it feels like."

Rage coiled tighter inside him. He hated that she'd known pain before and that she was experiencing it now. He hated the man who had done this to her and those who had forced her into such extreme circumstances. But more than anything, he was overwhelmed by the need to protect her. He wanted to be at her side for the rest of her life with his blade at the ready, prepared to slay any man who even thought of causing her pain.

"'Tis fine, Sutherland," she said.

He regulated his breathing to cool his ire and caught her sweet rose scent. It was delicate and fine, like her.

"'Tis no' fine." He curled his hand around hers, engulfing her slender, icy fingers. He wanted to embrace all of her thus. "Cormac. Please call me Cormac."

"Cormac," she whispered his name, her demeanor suddenly reticent.

He couldn't tear his gaze from the brilliance of her blue eyes. They were pale and flecked with green around her pupil, a color that reminded him of a summer loch. Heat effused his veins, and he found himself fighting the urge to pull her toward him to capture her mouth with his.

He gritted his teeth. He would do no such thing. Not when so many men had used her to their own advantage.

Except he was doing that very thing now too, was he not? He was seeking her hand in marriage so that he might have access to her wealth. His soul went dark with guilt. He should walk away, abandon the foolish notion of wooing her into marriage.

Graham appeared to be getting on well with Lady Clara. Surely, the dowry of one nobleman's daughter would be enough to sustain the clan until they managed a season of successful crops.

Cormac knew he should back away from her at that moment. Except her gaze swept to his mouth, her expression soft. Her hand was still in his, his large thumb tucked toward her palm with her fingers curled around his grip, holding him to her.

"Where else were ye injured?" he found himself asking.

She turned her face to the side, revealing a smear of blue at the edge of her jaw. "I concealed it with lily root powder at the feast."

It was not covered now. The mark was half the size of his smallest finger and ran along the sharp line of her jaw. His free hand raised of its own accord, and his fingertips whispered over the injury. Her skin was still damp from the rain and cool to the touch.

"Where else?" He asked.

She pulled her hand from his and gingerly touched her side, along the upper part of her waist near her ribs. "I don't need to bother with covering the bruise there." Her mouth quirked in a little smile he wanted to taste.

His hand settled there as well. He cradled her carefully with his fingertips by her waist and jaw. An ache settled within him, a powerful longing for this woman who had been left to care for herself when no one else would do so. A woman whose strength took her where a lady should not have to venture. A woman who had risen to the occasion regardless.

Her tongue ran along her lower lip, leaving it glistening with temptation, and her eyes found his once more. "Cormac," she said quietly.

"Isolde." Her name came out sounding gruff with the force of his need.

She edged closer to him, so her chest nearly grazed his. His heartbeat thundered in his ears and matched the pulse of desire in his groin. He should remove his hands from her, walk away and never look back.

She was not meant for Brodie, but nor was she meant for him. Not when he had need of her wealth. Not when he would be using her for land and coin as others in her life had.

He would not kiss her. Nor touch her. Nor long for her.

Then he made the mistake of looking into her eyes. Dark lashes rimmed such an exquisite blue that he felt himself tip into them and become lost with no desire to be found again. Her rose perfume intoxicated him like the strongest Highland whisky. Aye, he should leave, and yet he could not walk away.

What man could resist such alluring temptation?

⚜ 10 ⚜

I solde had never wanted to be kissed before. Men had tried in past years. Most of them idiots, their eyes bright with avarice.

But now—with Cormac's green gaze pulling her into the embrace of an abyss she never wanted to leave—now she wanted the press of his mouth against hers.

Kiss me.

She inched closer to him and tilted her chin upward, giving him easier access to her lips. His brows tensed as though he was in pain. Or mayhap warring with the decision.

Isolde had spent her life obeying the dictates of men. She'd been an obedient daughter and dutiful sister, and none of it had given her pleasure. Now, in a man's armor, defending her honor, she had created her path in life, forged with determination and the steel of her own convictions.

She put her hand on the thick fabric of his surcoat, pushed up on her toes and took the kiss he hesitated to give. His mouth was as warm as his hand had been, as soft as she had thought it might be.

She lingered there, savoring the press of their lips together, breathing in his spicy sandalwood and leather scent. His hand caressed the uninjured side of her face in a sensual stroke that teased down her neck and back up the underside of her chin. He cradled the back of her head in his palm and closed his mouth over hers.

Her heart slammed frantically at the nearness of him, at the way his lips moved over hers, at the brush of his tongue. Without realizing why, she parted her mouth for him. He deepened the kiss with his tongue, tasting her in an exquisite fashion that left her knees on the cusp of buckling.

She ran her hand down his surcoat, wishing he hadn't worn his gambeson and chainmail so that she might sense the bulk of his powerful body beneath. How she longed to feel his body through only a tunic or a linen.

Or perhaps nothing at all.

She could imagine it too easily, the heat of his skin against her touch, their bodies intimately close.

A steady pulse of need thrummed with insistence between her legs as their mouths parted and their tongues caressed. She arched against him in a desperate bid to alleviate her longing, but the clink of chainmail offered no respite.

His mouth slanted over hers with a low groan and pulled her more firmly against him. Their pelvises pushed against one another, yielding only pressure against the thick gambeson and impenetrable chain.

She gave a desperate whimper. Wanting more.

Her blood was impossibly hot as it raced through her veins like fire, and her thoughts fixated completely and totally on Cormac. On her desire for him.

He stepped away, panting. "We must stop." He rested his forehead against hers and closed his eyes.

"I don't want to," she murmured. She tilted her face toward him and nuzzled her nose to his so their lips whispered against one another.

His mouth touched hers in a firm kiss, as though he couldn't help himself any more than she could. Delicious chills raced over her skin.

He gave a low growl of an exhale. "We canna do this."

Isolde curled her arms over his neck. If her sensations were aflame despite so many layers, she could only imagine what they could experience without.

"Ye're shivering." He tenderly ran his thumb down her cheek and brushed away a damp bit of hair from her brow. "Ye need to return to the castle and put on a dry kirtle lest ye become ill."

She tucked her lip into her mouth as though she could capture the spicy taste of him and the thrilling feel of his kiss there forever. His attention dipped to her mouth. The thrum of desire pounded harder. He wanted to kiss her again as badly as she wished he would.

"Will you be at the joust?" she asked.

"Nay." He ran his hand through his hair. It was a casual gesture that left his black hair rumpled and boyishly endearing. "I need to gather some information during the joust."

Her fingers itched to smooth over the mussed tresses. "What sort of information?"

"On Brodie and the Ross clan."

Thoughts of Brodie invaded their cocoon of happiness like a draft of chilled air creeping beneath one's blankets. She scoffed. "What's he done this time?"

Cormac's jaw clenched, and she could tell he regretted having mentioned it.

Her curiosity piqued, she tilted her head. "What is it?"

"Isolde, ye must allow me to fight his champion for ye."

Isolde shook her head vehemently. "He might kill you."

Cormac stared at her, his expression fierce. "He *will* kill ye."

Isolde didn't argue. What could she possibly say when what he said was most likely the truth?

"Mayhap I could hire a champion of my own," she suggested.

"Can you recommend one?" While she had not taken many coins from Gilbert's coffers, she had enough of his finery to fetch a considerable sum.

"Ye have one right here." He lifted her hands in one of his. "And I'm better than anyone ye'll pay."

She loved the strength of his fingers curled around her own. Even as she relished his need to protect her, she hated what it might cost him. Tears warmed her eyes. "Your life is far dearer to me than any amount of coin."

He ran his thumb over the back of her hand. "I told ye that I would never leave ye unguarded. I stand by that vow. I will defend ye. I will fight Edmund the Braw for ye." He leveled his gaze with an earnestness that sank into her heart. "I will fight him, and I will win."

"I cannot discuss this any further." Isolde tugged her hands free of his grasp and pushed away from him. "I must go. They'll be expecting me at the joust given my absence previously." She paused at the tent flap and glanced at him. "I trust I'll see you at the feast?"

He inclined his head. "I'll be there."

Heat crept up her cheeks, but she didn't bother hiding her blush or how much pleasure she took from his words. She put the helm back on her head and slipped from the tent, rushing back to the castle.

Matilda had a fresh kirtle waiting for her as well as a roaring fire by which to dry her hair and quell the icy chill that had settled into her bones. Isolde stared into the flames as Matilda pulled the armor from her body and put a linen robe over her cold, wet skin.

In her mind, Isolde experienced Cormac's mouth on hers again, smooth and sensual. The heady rush of lust washed over her again, and she did not bother fighting the currents of its pull. She wanted every delicious moment of longing, eager for the moment it might be sated.

"My lady, you are by the fire too long," Matilda warned. "Your cheeks have gone red."

Isolde cast a shy glance at her maid. "'Tis thoughts of Cormac that flush my face so."

"Cormac?" Matilda lifted her brow as she carried over a fine blue-and-white kirtle.

Giddiness tickled inside Isolde's stomach. She didn't bother to smother her smile. "I mean Sutherland. The Chieftain of the Sutherland clan."

Matilda broke out in a wide grin. "He's been keen on you since our arrival, my lady."

"He knows our secret," Isolde whispered.

Matilda straightened, her expression going to one of concern.

"'Tis fine." Isolde put her back to her maid to be aided into the kirtle. "He wants to help us, but I think we might be able to help him as well." An idea was forming in Isolde's mind as her maid dressed her. There might be a way to prevent the fight with Brodie's champion.

Isolde slid her arm into the sleeve of her kirtle. The linen was wonderfully heated from where her maid had laid it by the fire. "I want you to listen to the talk at the joust today, Matilda. Especially to discussions of the men working for the knights in the tournament."

Matilda laced up the back of Isolde's kirtle with fast, expert fingers. "Of course, my lady. What is it you wish me to listen for?"

"The Ross clan is involved in some wrongdoing, I believe. I'd like to unearth what it might be."

Matilda gave a little gasp. "You think we might be able to have them removed from the tournament?"

Isolde nodded. "And if they can be removed from the tournament, we need not worry about Brodie's challenge or his champion at all."

It was a narrow chance, but it might be the only chance they had. For though she was well aware it might cause her death, she could not allow Cormac to fight Edmund the Braw in her stead.

※

THE MUD-SLICKED STREETS OF THE MARKET WERE FILLED WITH gossip. Cormac meandered through the vendors with his senses on alert for any new information. There was much to be had—how Laurence de Govic won all the jousts the prior day and how the first night of the feast Sir Alexander de Mandeville had Elinor of York sit beside him rather than her own father who was six seats away. Despite the wagging tongues, the subjects all pertained to people Cormac didn't know and events he had little care for.

Not when he needed information on the Rosses. He'd sent Duncan, Lachlan and Alan to the jousting lists where they might have better luck. Cormac only hoped they would have more success than what he'd uncovered thus far.

A woman in a wide-brimmed hat strode by with a tray of apples and paused in front of Cormac, her brow lifted in a silent question that could be taken as an offer for an apple or something more. Cormac shook his head and turned away. Even before meeting Isolde, he never fell prey to such temptations.

And after Isolde...

After her, he could scarcely think at all. Not without imagining how her kiss-reddened lips had felt beneath his mouth or how she'd stared at him with her heavy-lidded blue eyes. Desire swept through him and left him hot with distraction.

Pain burst at the back of his head. He spun about with his hand pressed to the offending point of impact on his skull. A damaged apple rolled away from him.

Irate, he snapped his head up, half-expecting to find the suggestive apple seller prepared to lob another bit of fruit his way. Instead, he found Graham standing there, green eyes twinkling with good humor. "I tried calling out to ye." His brother lifted his shoulders as if that were excuse enough.

"And now ye've wasted food when our people are starving." Cormac pulled his hand away from his head, bringing a small chunk of white apple flesh with it.

"Ach, 'tis fine." Graham picked up the apple and held it into the rain until all the mud had washed away. "Save the part ye ruined with yer head."

"Where have ye been?" Cormac asked in a gruff tone. "I know ye come to the tent because ye're still sleeping when I leave in the morn. Then ye're gone when I'm back at noon and dinna return until after I'm asleep."

Graham rubbed the apple on his tunic and bit into it. "I've been occupied."

"Lady Clara?" Cormac asked in a low tone.

Hope rose in Cormac's chest. Their people needed at least one fortune to save them. If Graham was having success with Lady Clara, Cormac could leave off Isolde.

Guilt tugged at him once more. She'd been preyed upon by many men who sought to use her dowry and noble position to their own advantage. Yet, even as he wrestled with the dilemma of hurting her, he was all too keenly aware of his people's starvation. Was it worth another clansman's life to keep from hurting her?

"How do ye fare with Lady Clara?" Cormac pressed.

Graham winced. "I canna say. The lass is too hard to read. Every time I get close, she pulls away." He smirked indulgently. "I'm rather having fun with it all."

Bitter disappointment turned in Cormac's gut.

"Ye're having fun while our people starve." Cormac led Graham to the awning of a thatch-roofed home where he could speak to his brother in relative privacy and without exposure to the rain.

"Ye say that as though ye're no' doing the same." Graham lifted his brows. "How do ye fare with Lady Isolde? It appears that ye've been getting on with her verra well. I believe I saw ye dancing with her the other night?"

"I wouldna call what I was doing dancing," Cormac muttered. "More like I followed her instruction while she tried to guide me through a dance with steps I dinna know."

Graham laughed. "I wasna going to mention it, but now that ye've brought it up..."

If Cormac wasn't in such a foul mood, he might have laughed at his brother's jest, but his irritation left him glowering instead.

"So, it isna going well then?" Graham asked in a discouraged tone.

"Nay." Cormac sighed. "'Tis going verra well."

Graham watched the people of the market duck to avoid the steady rainfall that came down with a vengeance. "Going verra well should be a good thing, aye?"

Cormac didn't bother moving his feet back from the splashing runoff. There was no point when he was already so drenched.

"I've learned more about her," Cormac answered. "Men have sought her out for their personal gain through her noble birth." He paused. "And her wealth." He clenched his fist to stave off the blow of guilt, though it did little good. "She's been hurt and abandoned, even by her own brother."

Graham lifted a brow. "Was that no' her brother fighting for her honor?"

Cormac shook his head, not willing to share Isolde's secrets. "'Tis a long story."

"And ye dinna care for her?" Graham asked. "She's bonny enough."

"Aye, she is." Cormac's blood turned hot as he recalled how she'd looked in his tent, her brother's armor and sodden gambeson, her lips and chin red from their kisses. "I care for her too much. I dinna want to hurt her."

"And how would ye be hurting her?" Graham took another bite of the apple and studied Cormac while he chewed.

The band of tension around Cormac's chest squeezed even tighter. "If I marry her for her wealth, then I'm as bad as every other man who has sought her hand. If I use her for her power, I'm no better than her brother."

Graham's eyes were crinkled with amusement.

"Why are ye looking at me like that?" Cormac demanded.

Graham crossed his arms over his chest, with one still cradling the apple and leaned on the wall, so he faced Cormac. "Like what?"

"Like ye find me amusing."

"I do find ye amusing." Graham put a finger to his chin in exaggerated concentration. "What if ye dinna have to worry about the clan?"

"I always have to worry about the clan."

Graham put up his hands to stop Cormac from speaking. "What if ye dinna have to worry about the clan and ye had met Lady Isolde here? Would ye consider marriage to her?"

Cormac regarded his brother for a long, stupefied moment. The idea of how *he* felt about marriage to Isolde had not entered his mind. Not when it had been so full of that kiss. And not when he'd been so plagued with guilt.

Generally, Cormac overthought everything, looking at it from all angles before finally settling on the safest option.

But everything had happened so quickly: learning about what occurred in Isolde's past, feeling so protective of her, the passion they'd shared. He hadn't had time to analyze it until that very moment when he'd been asked to do so.

Could he see himself wed to Isolde?

He could imagine her in his bed, that much he knew with certainty. Her body, lean from her efforts in training with a sword, naked and writhing under his touch.

He nudged his thoughts away, lest he end up with a cockstand. It was not difficult to picture Isolde by his side, a warrior queen. The perfect wife for a chieftain. A woman who would hold her own, earn the respect of the clan and be a mother who would defend their bairns with the ferocity of a lioness.

Graham pushed off the wall and clapped Cormac on the shoulder. "I dinna think ye're going to be using her like ye think." He poked a finger into Cormac's chest. "Ye've got the look of a man in love."

In love?

Cormac scoffed, unwilling to even consider this latest claim.

"'Tis a better start than most marriages get." Graham bit into the apple again and strode off toward the center of the market while offering a farewell wave over his shoulder.

Cormac watched his departure. Graham wasn't always right, but on the matter of a marriage to Isolde, he might well be. Cormac left the marketplace and headed in the direction of his tent to prepare for the feast later on that night.

Once more, his focus flitted to Isolde. Her smile, her strength, her beauty and her determination. God's teeth, never had there existed such a woman as she.

Was he in love?

Nay. Certainly not.

But he did care for the lass.

Additionally, Graham was correct in noting it was more than most marriages began with. The idea of mutual compatibility with Isolde eased the pressure of Cormac's guilt. After all, with a woman who appealed to him in so many ways, Cormac could be certain he was not wanting to be with her for her wealth, but for the life that they might share with mutual joy, passion and respect.

Such thoughts sealed his decision, and he knew with certainty what he needed to do.

That night, following the feast, he would ask Lady Isolde to be his wife.

I solde settled herself on a cushion in the stands as the jousters were preparing themselves on their horses. The rain continued to come down in earnest, though the awning over the stands kept the observers dry. At least those fortunate enough to not be on the ground. Peasants were left to crowd behind the wooden barrier beneath the open sky, ignoring the rain in exchange for such fine entertainment.

Isolde was just as eager to be in attendance. Now that Cormac knew she did not shy from combat, she did not have to feign disgust in the joust.

She cast a glance at her maid. "Matilda, please fetch me a goblet of wine."

Matilda offered a slight curtsy. "Of course, my lady."

She departed and would not return for some time. Not that anybody would notice. Isolde returned her attention to the jousters as the pair prepared to charge.

Thomas Brisbois of Kelso's chainmail was muddy from his previous joust, but he was now donning a fresh surcoat, the green and white vivid against his dirty armor. He settled the lance in his arm, and the horses charged at one another, their hooves throwing up globs of mud as they ran. They collided in a spray of splinters as their lances broke against the other.

The joust was a long one, made grueling by the unfortunate weather. As Isolde observed the sport, she listened to the conversations around her. There were details about the jousts that day, of course. Apparently, several horses spooked earlier during a particularly nasty bit of the storm, and in his joust with Sir Julian, Sir Edward broke his leg when his horse fell on him.

No other pertinent information drifted from the surrounding nobles. Certainly nothing about the Ross clan. But then, that would most likely come from Matilda. Servants had more salacious gossip than their masters.

A large man pushed through the crowd of peasants, shoving people from his path as he went. Though many gave cries of offense, none challenged his presence. In fact, most darted out of his way rather than be removed by force.

The man was two heads taller than most, his face set in a darkened scowl, his shoulders as solid as a great stone and spanning just as wide. He was more beast than man. A shiver ran down Isolde's back.

"Is that him?" the woman behind Isolde asked.

Isolde leaned in her seat along with several other people to watch as he disappeared under the stands.

"Aye," her companion replied. "No one has ever been able to defeat Edmund the Braw."

Ice chilled Isolde's veins. That massive beast of a man was Edmund the Braw?

Her breath came short. No one had told her he hadn't been defeated. She wouldn't last minutes fighting against a man such as him. Cormac would last longer, but...

Undefeated.

Isolde pressed her hand to her chest as though she could return the panicked beat of her heart to its normal pace.

Moments later, Matilda arrived with a goblet of wine in her

hand. "Forgive me, my lady, for it took some time to find the particular wine I know you prefer."

Isolde accepted the goblet and gave her maid a knowing look. "Please tell me you were able to get exactly what I asked for?"

Matilda nodded solemnly. "Indeed, I did, my lady."

Isolde's pulse tripped over itself with relief. Matilda had found something.

Mayhap the information could prove Brodie was up to something nefarious. If Isolde could expose him to Lord Yves, it might be so bad that he would be placed under arrest and she wouldn't have to fight his champion. She wouldn't have to ensure Cormac did not take her place. With trembling fingers, she brought the wine to her numb lips and took a sip.

She wanted to leave the joust and seek privacy to find out exactly what Matilda had learned. If it was something that would spare her the fight, they would need to begin planning immediately.

After several sips of wine that she could not taste, Isolde handed the goblet back to Matilda. "I'm afraid all this rain has given me quite a headache. I should like to retire."

Matilda immediately stood. "Of course, my lady."

Together, they left the stands and began the slow walk toward the castle. This time, both women were armed with daggers. The Rosses would not catch them off guard again.

The journey back to the castle was uneventful. Thanks be to God.

"The news I bear is not as you think," Matilda said in a low tone meant only for Isolde.

Isolde held out a hand to stop her maid from speaking further. "Say nothing until we return to our chambers."

She knew all too well exactly who could be listening. She didn't want the Ross clan to have any knowledge of what she had gleaned lest they try to thwart her plans. She couldn't afford any opportunity to be ruined.

As soon as the door to Isolde's rooms were closed, she looked to her maid. "What is it? What did you find?"

Matilda's expression crumpled. "I'm afraid 'tis not good news."

Isolde's heart squeezed. "Tell me."

"The Ross clan is involved in a plot to overthrow King Richard."

Isolde had been right. The Rosses were involved in something terrible. Her mind immediately raced with what she could do with such information. Surely, Lord Yves would have the Ross clan arrested.

"This is excellent news," she exclaimed.

Matilda appeared chagrined. "They are involved due to an agreement with an English noble." She looked down at her feet and spoke the most awful words. "The Earl of Easton."

The air sucked out of Isolde's chest. "My brother? Gilbert?"

Matilda gave a slow nod. "It is why he allowed Brodie time alone with you and how he was in the area to find you together..." She swallowed. "...As he did."

Isolde shook her head, aghast.

Gilbert was involved in the plot. He was committing high treason. He would be ruined. They would lose everything.

Her emotions reeled through so many layers of heartbreak and disappointment. This might have been her one opportunity to escape from the challenge Brodie had issued. But she could not go to Lord Yves to report Brodie's nefarious deeds. For her brother—and she—would also be implicated.

The back of her throat ached with the threat of tears. "This can't be."

Matilda approached Isolde and took her hand as she continued. "The land in your dowry once belonged to the Ross clan. They've been trying to reclaim it for decades. Lord Easton knew this and realized what an advantage they could be when he proposed the idea."

Humiliation washed over Isolde. "Servants know far too much." And it made Isolde suddenly feel like the greatest fool.

"'Tis why you sent me," Matilda replied gently.

A hot tear trailed down Isolde's cheek, and she nodded. Matilda was correct. It was why Isolde had sent her. Servants were silent observers to all that went on around them. It did not mean they never spoke of what had been witnessed. Especially when given proper motivation. Like a lovely lady's maid who gave them her full attention.

Isolde nodded. "Please go on." When Matilda did not immediately continue, Isolde glanced up at her maid. "There is more, is there not?"

Matilda pressed her lips together and nodded. "My lord knew you would decline any offer of marriage to Brodie, and intentionally put you in a position where you had no choice but to accept."

"By tarnishing my honor." An angry sob erupted from deep within Isolde. "My own brother betrayed me to get the support he needed to engage in treason. He sacrificed me intentionally for his own gain. Not just me, but my integrity."

The news shattered her heart. She had known her brother did not hold much love for her. But what he'd done had been cruel. Beyond cruel. It had been wholly self-serving and hateful.

The worst part of all was that there was no solution now to avoid the challenge Brodie had laid at her feet. She would still need to fight Edmund the Braw. And she would certainly lose.

❦

CORMAC WAS NO LONGER PLAGUED BY GUILT REGARDING Isolde. Not since he made up his mind about his intentions.

Especially when he knew she was not inclined to wed Brodie. The very thought of the man left Cormac scowling. And, frustratingly, neither he nor any of his men had any luck with uncovering more information about the Ross clan's involvement with an attempt to overthrow the rightful king of England.

Though Cormac tried to push away such thoughts, he could not help but be burdened by them as he dressed with great care for the feast that evening. It wasn't until he caught sight of Isolde across the Great Hall that all thoughts of Brodie completely fled Cormac's mind.

For how could he even think of the rival clan, or anyone else for that matter, when his gaze fell on such beauty? Her auburn hair was bound back in a single braid with slight wisps framing her face. She hadn't seen him yet, and he used that moment to study her.

Her head was tilted at a slight angle as though in considera-tion. Her blue gaze swept toward him as he approached and held. All at once, a smile of recognition lit her face and warmed in his chest. Matilda offered him a curtsey from where she stood behind the seat next to her mistress, clearly holding it for him.

He nodded his thanks to her maid and took the saved seat. Isolde's rose scent teased at his memories, igniting the heat of passion anew. His arms ached to curl around her, and he longed for the caress of her sweet lips.

He sank into the seat and drew her hand to his mouth for a kiss. It was a courtier's move, one he'd seen Graham use on ladies. It was never one he had thought he would personally indulge. Until Isolde.

"I have news to share with you," she said in a voice low enough to fade into the din around them. "I cannot say it here."

Cormac nodded, grateful they would have cause to leave the feast and a chance to be alone so that he might ask for her hand in marriage.

For the time they were there, however, he was content to be at Isolde's side amid the other attendees. The blanket of awkward-ness he'd always harbored around women seemed to fall away as he jested with her and enjoyed the easy flow of conversation between them. Every now and then, however, he would catch flashes of tension in her eyes.

That was what brought the most concern. Whatever she needed to tell him, away from prying eyes, was most assuredly not good.

The feast finally ended with their stomachs full of hearty food. Tables were pushed aside for dancing, a perfect opportunity to lead her from the Great Hall to somewhere they might speak privately. "Lady Isolde, I believe the rain has finally stopped falling." He extended his arm to her. "Would ye, and yer maid, of course, care to join me for a walk?"

Isolde flushed and slid her hand in the crook of his arm. He loved how she gently rested her hand on his forearm, featherlight.

Cormac led her from the Great Hall outside, beyond the servant's tables and to the outskirts of the village with Matilda several paces behind, her presence to ensure no one overheard their conversation more so than to protect her mistress's virtue.

Isolde gazed up at him, beautiful in the wash of moonlight. Her skin gleamed like a pearl, and her auburn hair shone with a luxurious sheen. "I had Matilda ask about the Ross clan during the joust today."

Cormac ground his teeth in frustration at himself. He never should have mentioned looking into the Ross clan to her. Of course, she went of her own volition to see what she could uncover. "And ye found something?"

Isolde nodded. "Aye, they are planning to overthrow King Richard."

Shite.

Cormac sighed. "I hadna wanted ye to know."

Someone shouted in the distance followed by the raucous laughter of men. Cormac stepped closer to ensure their speech would not be overheard.

"That was not all Matilda discovered." Isolde bit her lip, and her eyes went glossy with unshed tears.

Cormac reached for her and gently held her slender arms in his hands. "What is it?"

"'Tis not the Ross clan who is behind the coup." Isolde sighed. "'Tis my brother."

Cormac didn't speak for one stunned moment. "How did ye learn of this? I sent Alan to gather information as well, and he heard none of this. Nor did either of my other two men."

"Alan is not as beautiful as Matilda." Isolde lifted a brow. "I cannot imagine your other men are either."

He tipped his head in surrender. "People dinna trust the Scottish enough to divulge their secrets to Lachlan and Duncan. Alan has a better chance of that when it comes to the English." The latter part held more truth than Cormac cared to admit. It was why he continued to employ Alan. "But beauty does have a means of moving the most stoic of men."

Her distress cleared as she gazed into his eyes. "Does it?"

"Pip isna my dog," Cormac confessed.

Isolde gave a quiet laugh. "I know."

"Marry me, Isolde." The suddenness of his request surprised even him. "Here. Tonight. Let me take ye from all of this. If ye're wed to me, ye willna be free to marry Brodie. We'll be bound together by God."

Her smile faded into a frown of concentrated thought.

"Ye've been ignored by men who should have protected ye for too long." He closed the scant distance between them and caressed the softness of her cheek. "I canna stop thinking of ye. No' since the first moment I saw ye, when I thought ye were the bonniest lass I'd ever laid eyes on."

"Did you?" Her blush was evident even in the low light.

"Aye." His fingertips brushed just beneath her lips. God's Teeth, how he longed to kiss her. "But ye're no' just bonny. Ye're brave, determined, strong." He shook his head. "There's no' a lass like ye in the world. And I'd rather die than lose ye to a man like Brodie Ross who sorely does not deserve ye."

She shuddered at his words and started to shake her head, no doubt to tell him she would not allow him to take her place in the challenge.

"Ye've always been poorly cared for." Cormac drew his arms around her, securing her to him. "For the rest of our lives, let me protect ye. Let me love ye."

The last bit had not been intended. But he did not regret it. For there in the empty moonlit field, with her in his embrace and gazing up at him as though he were the only man in the world, he had never wanted anything more than Isolde Maxwell as his wife.

Was he in love?

His finger traced over her full lower lip, and she drew in a soft breath.

Possibly.

"Will ye?" he asked when she did not answer. "Will ye marry me?"

❦ 12 ❧

For the first time in Isolde's life, someone was truly seeing her. Not as a source of wealth or a means of advancing their status, but her as a woman. Not once had Cormac mentioned her dowry. Indeed, he had even asked her to marry him after she had confessed that her brother was a traitor.

And he wanted to protect her. Evidence of his intention was not only in the earnestness of his words but in the strong, warm circle of his arms. He made her feel safe.

In all of Isolde's life, no one had ever sought to save her. Her father had focused all his attention on Gilbert, his prized son, who would carry on the name and title. Once Gilbert assumed the earldom, he had cared for her only in how her future union could give him a powerful alliance.

Earlier that evening, before the feast, the servant from her home that she had paid to inform her of Gilbert's well-being had finally arrived. He informed her that her brother was well after several days of being terribly ill. And that he was furious.

However, he no longer considered her to be his problem, but Brodie Ross's, and would leave her to him so long as she returned Gilbert's clothing posthaste. Isolde complied, but intentionally omitted his armor. After all, she did have need of it the following day. He could do whatever he liked with it when she was dead.

The thought was a sobering one, which recalled the severity of the situation she still faced.

"I do not know if I will live past tomorrow," Isolde said with sincerity. "But I do truly wish to marry you."

Cormac gave her a wide grin that put his dimple on full display. "Ye needn't worry about fighting Edmund the Braw anymore. I'll be fighting in your stead." Before she could open her mouth, he put a finger to her lips to still her protest. "Ye'll be my wife, and I protect what's mine."

Isolde shook her head. "Nay, I cannot allow you—"

"I will keep ye safe no matter the cost." He leveled his stare to meet hers, his words brimming with conviction.

"I cannot lose you." The words caught in her throat. "There must be another way."

He pulled her more firmly against him, drawing her to the wall of his powerful body. She nestled into him and breathed in his wonderfully masculine scent.

"We will think on it more in the morning," he said into her ear. "Come, let us find a priest and be wed before anyone can try to stop us."

Giddiness rushed through Isolde as she took Cormac's offered hand. "Come be our witness, Matilda," she called out to her maid. "We are to be wed."

If Matilda had any reservations about the abruptness of her mistress's decision, they were well hidden in the beaming smile. Together, Isolde and Cormac ran like children toward the heart of the village, their hands enfolded in one another's.

Surely, a priest could be found at such an hour.

In Isolde's younger days, when she'd always done as she was supposed to, she had never been impulsive. Now, in the span of only four days, she had poisoned her brother, stolen his armor to wear as she pretended to be him, fought for her own honor and won, and was now agreeing to wed a man she'd known only days. But her choices were ones she had made, without anyone's permission but her own. It had all been liberating and empowering.

They slowed to a walk as they came to the village and looked at each other with joyfully shared laughter while they waited for Matilda to join them.

"Promise me something," Isolde said.

"Anything." It was in the earnest manner he readily agreed as well as the adoration evident in his eyes that Isolde knew he meant it. She could ask him for the very moon at that moment, and he would ensure she had it in her hands anon.

"Promise me you'll never fill my life with rules and that I may continue to train with my sword." Her words came out breathless from the exertion of their sprint and the force of her own excitement.

He held her face between his large hands. "I promise." His mouth pressed to hers.

Isolde tilted her chin to better enjoy the kiss. She had been simmering with lust throughout the day at the recollections of their last one, of how he had awoken within her a burning need. Her tongue teased over his lips and they parted to allow his tongue to stroke against hers.

A groan sounded in his throat and sent ripples of pleasure prickling over her skin. She curled her arms around the back of his neck and pressed as close to him as possible, deepening the kiss as they had done earlier that day.

He nudged her back against the nearby hut, pushing her into it with his body. Brodie had done similar, although he had been forceful in his efforts, and such attention had been unwelcome. With Cormac, she wanted to part her legs and feel the full force of his desire against her most intimate place.

"A priest," he growled against her lips. "We need a priest." He pushed off of her and held out his hand, his chest rising and falling with the quickening of his breath.

A glance back at the field surrounding the village confirmed Matilda was nearly to them.

Isolde's fingers shook with anticipation as she set them to his palm and allowed him to lead her into the heart of the village. It was difficult to walk at a steady pace when such a bone-melting kiss had weakened her knees.

Procuring a priest amidst a tournament had seemed an easy enough task. However, it proved to be a difficult feat. One that appeared impossible.

The first two had been found in the taverns, slobbering over serving wenches and so ripe with drink, their words were incoherent. Even if they could recall the wedding vows, it was doubtful they would be understood. One of them had at least pointed in the direction of a man who might help.

They found him rushing through the village. He took one look at their clasped hands and gave an exasperated sigh. "Another union in a hurry?" He looked upward as though seeking God's agreement at the incredulity. "These tournaments are preposterous with so many rushed weddings."

"Will ye be free to wed us?" Cormac asked.

"Not tonight," the priest replied in a brusque tone.

"Is there another priest then?" Isolde asked in a rush of desperation.

He shook his head. "There are only three of us, and someone's already enlisted my services. I take it that the other two were already sotted?"

Isolde nodded and tried to suppress her disappointment, for it weighed as heavy upon her as a millstone.

His severe expression softened, and she could see that he was actually quite young. "I've no plans on the morrow," he replied. "I can marry you then. After the feast."

Isolde's heart slid into her stomach. There were too many things that could go horribly wrong in the morning. When the fight against Brodie's impossible champion ensued. There may not be a tomorrow.

"We'll see ye after the feast on the morrow," Cormac said confidently.

The priest nodded and dashed off, muttering to himself. Matilda kept her distance in order to allow Isolde the opportunity to speak candidly with Cormac.

Isolde clasped his hand more tightly. "That is too late."

He shook his head. "Nay, my love. We will wed tomorrow. I will defeat—"

She pressed her mouth to his to still his words. Her heart could not bear to have that conversation again. How could she allow him to fight Edmund? Especially after she'd seen that great hulking beast of a man.

Undefeated.

How could either of them possibly win?

She didn't want to think about any of it. "Bed me tonight," she said between kisses.

He pulled back and regarded her with uncertainty.

She ran her hand over his cheek, and the short stubble rasped over her fingertips. "No one need to know the priest cannot do it tonight. We'll be wed tomorrow but can tell everyone we are man and wife already, especially once I've been bedded."

He was beginning to shake his head, but she caught his face between her hands to stop the action. "My honor is already in question. If I'm to be judged for something I did not do, I might as well enjoy it." Despite her bold words, a hot blush stole over her chest and face. "With the man I will soon wed."

He frowned, apparently not liking the idea.

"Please," she whispered. "Is that not what you say when I've told you 'nay?'"

"I'm no' saying 'nay .'"

Isolde bit her lip to still the widening of her smile. "Then I will take that as an 'aye.'"

HOW COULD CORMAC POSSIBLY REFUSE ISOLDE'S REQUEST WHEN she gazed at him thus? Her eyes were bright with hope; her mouth still red from their kisses; her cheeks flushed with excitement and desire. He would take her here and now if he could.

After all, they would be wed on the morrow.

He cradled her face. "Aye," he replied gruffly as he lowered his lips to hers once more.

He could spend a lifetime kissing her in the middle of the village, his body hot with the flames of lust. Thunder rumbled overhead, and rain began to spatter out of the clouds in a mist that warned of an oncoming storm.

She leaned her head back and smiled coyly at him. "Come to my rooms at the castle."

He hesitated. He would be having her before they were wed. His father would roll in his grave at the idea of Cormac even considering taking a lady's innocence without first being her husband.

She laughed at Cormac's delayed reply. "We cannot very well go to your tent."

"Isolde, mayhap we ought to—"

The mirth dimmed from her eyes, and she shook her head. "Please don't change your mind."

He went quiet, unable to speak what they both were thinking. As confident as he was in his own ability to fight, it did not eliminate the possibility that he might soon die. If he got her with child...

She put her hand in his once more, wrapping her tapered fingers around his wide palm. "Come." She tugged at him in an effort to lead him toward the castle. Toward her bedchamber.

He allowed her to pull him toward the Rose Citadel, but as they neared, he drew back. "Have Matilda find a servant to fetch me. I'll no' have someone see ye leading me to yer rooms."

She nodded and let her gaze slide down his body in a way that left a lingering burn humming over his skin before she disappeared into the castle. Several minutes later, after the bells of the curfew had rung out, Alan approached with a grin on his face and Pip trotting at his side.

"Matilda found me and bade me show you to her rooms." Alan lifted his brows in a suggestive gesture.

"And ye know where they are?" Cormac folded his arms over his chest.

Pip stood before Cormac, wagging his tail so ferociously that it made his whole body rock from side to side. Cormac sighed and crouched down to pet the beast.

"I've gone all through the castle." Alan shrugged. "'Tis part of my job to know who is who and where they are. I figured you'd especially like to know the location of Lady Isolde's room should trouble arise. Especially with the likes of the Rosses."

Cormac gave a final pat to Pip's velvety head and straightened, nodding at Alan's foresight. The man might have injected himself into Cormac's life, but he was helpful to have about.

Alan bowed and gestured for Cormac to follow him. "Your lady awaits."

His lady.

His pulse quickened to think of her in her private rooms, waiting for him. The woman he would marry.

The threat of Edmund edged into his thoughts, but he shoved that away. After all, Cormac had plans for the following morning. While Alan led him through the castle and up to Isolde, Cormac shared what he had in mind and ordered Alan to speak with Matilda and ensure all was handled accordingly.

"It will be done, sir." Alan inclined his head and indicated the door in front of them as they came to a stop.

Cormac rapped softly on the heavy wood, and Matilda appeared. Pip craned his neck to look into the room, but Alan immediately sank to his knees and held his dog back. Matilda smiled at the dog and his master as she slipped from the chamber and allowed Cormac to enter.

He pushed the door closed behind him to enter the receiving room. Dark, heavy wood chairs with plush, red velvet padding sat near a fireplace, and a chest of drawers filled the small room. One door off to the side was cracked open with the golden glow of candlelight just beyond. His pulse hammered in his veins, and he walked silently over the thickly woven carpet to where he knew he would find Isolde.

He entered the room and drew up short at the sight before him. Isolde stood before the fire, her hair unbound and falling around her in auburn waves, wearing only a silken robe tied at the waist. It didn't show any more flesh than the gowns she usually wore, mayhap even less. But her hardened nipples pebbled beneath the rich fabric.

"I feared you might not come," Isolde said in a low voice, silky and intimate.

He swallowed and pushed the bolt on the door, locking it.

"Do you want some wine?" She approached a small table with a decanter and two pewter chalices. Without waiting for an answer, she lifted the wine, accidentally knocking one of the goblets over.

Despite her eagerness, she was obviously nervous. As any maiden would be. How he wished that he possessed Graham's ease with women. What Cormac knew very well, however, was how he felt about her.

He joined her by the table and straightened the goblet. "I dinna need wine." He took her slender hand in his. "Ye're all the intoxication I need."

"Me?" Isolde flushed. "Intoxicating?"

He gently stroked the knuckle of his forefinger down her cheek. "We dinna have to do this now, lass. We can wait—"

"For the morrow?" Her eyes filled with tears. "I saw Edmund the Braw at the joust."

Cormac had seen Brodie's champion before and knew how his presence alone could intimidate. "Then ye understand why I'm insisting on going in yer stead."

Her eyes widened. "He's undefeated. You could be—"

"I willna," Cormac said.

"You could be killed," Isolde said.

Cormac poured her a goblet of wine and handed it to her, but she did not drink it. "I will do anything to keep ye safe, Isolde."

"And I you." She set aside her wine and reached for him with both hands.

He came to her and pulled her into his arms. Her robe was slippery under his hands, her curves naked beneath.

"I wish we could leave here," she whispered.

Except there were too many complications and they both knew it. The Ross clan would go after Cormac, or Lord Easton, or Cormac *and* Isolde. This feud would not be over until it had been handled properly, and Cormac refused to start his marriage to Isolde on the run.

He brushed the top of her head with his lips. Her hair was cool and smooth like her robe. He put his fingertips to the underside of her chin and tipped her face up so he could meet her eyes. "Think only of our wedding tomorrow and nothing else."

A slow smile spread over her lips. "There may be more for us to think about."

His blood immediately went hot, and he lifted a brow in silent question.

She draped her arms around the back of his neck and rose up on her toes, so her body pressed to his. It was all the invitation he needed. He held her to him and lowered his mouth to hers, ready to claim her as his wife.

❧ 13 ❧

Isolde would convey with her body what her mouth could not to Cormac. That she could not allow him to sacrifice himself for her. That she preferred to spend this last night being alive in his arms. That even if she was found out and forced to marry Brodie, she needed at least this memory to carry her through the rest of her days of misery bound to a man she did not want.

She gathered the ferocity of her emotions and poured it all into her passion. Her mouth explored the warmth of his as she brazenly licked his lower lip, enticing him to deepen their kiss.

His hands ran through her hair, which sent up wafts of rose-water blooming from her long tresses.

"Ye smell so good," he groaned. His mouth traveled down her jaw to her neck, the scrape of his unshaven chin sending delicious prickles of pleasure dancing through her. His kisses shifted lower and brushed over her collarbone where her pulse no doubt thudded with the force of a blacksmith's hammer.

She reached for him as he kissed her body, desperate to feel all of him this time, not the hint of sensations through so many layers of metal and thick cloth but skin to skin. His hands glided down her silk robe as he explored the curves of her body with strong, sure hands. Her skin tingled with the most exquisite awareness so that every stroke of his hand left a humming sensation in its wake.

She ran her fingers over his tunic, sampling the strength of his torso from atop his clothing. His muscles were solid under her exploration. Masculine. Perfect.

His fingertips whispered against the sides of her breasts, and a moan escaped from her throat. He leaned back slightly to watch her as his thumb brushed over her nipple. She sucked in a sharp inhale of delight. A throb of desire began at her core, its tune coming in pulses of need.

In a slow, careful move, he nudged aside the lapel of her robe to display one breast. Her cheeks burned with shyness, and she lowered her gaze to avoid watching his reaction. Instead, her focus fell on his large hand as he cupped her with great care, setting her skin aflame with such intimacy. His thumb swept over the bud of her nipple and circled it with a delicate touch that made her heart gallop. The little pink nub drew tight with pleasure.

"Ye're so verra beautiful, Isolde." Cormac reached for the length of silk belting her waist and pulled.

The bow she had hastily tied while rushing to prepare for Cormac's arrival slipped free and cool air whispered over her skin. His gaze dipped to the gap where her body was visible between the blue silk.

He slid his hand beneath the robe to her bare skin. The contact of his fingers on her nakedness jolted through her with a crackle of energy so great that it made her gasp. His caress brushed her back first, sending a series of decadent shivers down her spine, then lowered to the curve of her bottom as he drew her closer to him.

His mouth met hers with a fierce hunger that burned through her reticence and heightened her desire. Their kisses turned frantic as they panted between suckles and licks. He kissed down her neck, his chin rasping her sensitive skin while his soft lips continued to worship her.

His hands were both on her bottom, fitting their bodies together, pelvis to pelvis as they moved in lustful tandem. She grasped the hem of his tunic and pulled it upward. He released her and pulled the garment over his head, followed by the linen beneath. He stood before her, chest rising and falling with his heavy breathing.

She'd known he was strong but had been ill-prepared for the powerful lines of his chest and rippled stomach, and how muscle truly could sculpt the body as surely as a chisel set to marble. His gaze raked down her body to where the gap of her robe had widened.

Knowing exactly what she wanted and willing to do everything she could to get it, she shrugged out of the robe and let it fall to the floor. Only then did she remember the bruises on her body from her fight with Brodie. They would be unseemly. Decidedly not ladylike. But his green stare did not hover over her ribs or her arm.

Nay, it raked over all of her with desire, and she knew that despite her injuries, he found her desirable.

It was she who closed the distance between them while he remained in place as he stared. She pressed her body against his, so the dark sprinkling of hair on his chest prickled against her sensitive nipples. He studied her with an intensity that made her wonder if he was memorizing every inch of her. Still watching her, he sank down to his knees and parted his lips over her left nipple.

His tongue flicked against the little pink nub before drawing it into the wet heat of his mouth. She cried out and clung to his broad shoulders to keep from sliding to the floor. One strong arm tightened around her while the other caressed and teased over her other breast.

The whole world seemed to melt around her as his tongue

swirled against her nipple. He switched to her other breast as his hand went first to her waist, then her hips, then slowly, tantalizingly, toward the apex of her thighs where lust pulsed hot with ravenous need.

His hand hovered there, stretching out time for one heart-stopping moment before letting his touch sweep over the cleft between her legs. He straightened and kissed her mouth as he stroked her most intimate place.

She shook with overwhelming pleasure as his tongue brushed hers. His incredible fingers slid over her sex, settling at the apex where the most exquisite bliss made her tremble. She moaned against his lips and arched closer. Wanting more.

Desperate for all of him.

His fingertips probed against her and eased inside carefully while he continued to administer small, maddening circles to the bud of her sex. Her breath came out in hard pants, and tension tightened through her core. All at once, and much to her great disappointment, he removed his hand from her. She whimpered in protest, but he swept her into the strength of his muscular arms and carried her to the massive bed where he lay her atop the velvet coverlet.

Her body was on fire for him, trembling with anticipation. He stretched over her, his bare chest grazing against her hardened nipples. He kissed her lips first, then her neck, followed by her breasts. She rubbed her thighs together to still the aching lust, but it only served to make her more desperate for his touch.

He continued downward, crawling backward as he did so, his mouth at her ribs, then her navel, then...

He spread her thighs with gentle hands and lowered his head to her sex. Isolde gasped sharply. Mortification. Shock. Pleasure. Oh, such pleasure as his wicked tongue flicked out and licked between her thighs. Heat tingled through her palms and feet and traveled inward to tighten at her core.

Everything within her seemed to vibrate with enough force to make her shatter. She grabbed the coverlet beneath her, and suddenly the tension exploded into total euphoria that left white stars blooming behind her eyelids.

When she opened her eyes again, Cormac was grinning up at her. He slowly eased off the bed and untied the band around his waist. His eyes were like firelit emeralds, bright with desire and fixed on her as he slid his hose to the ground, revealing his powerful thighs sprinkled with dark hair. Between his legs was a patch of black hair with a column of flesh jutting from it, hard and pulsing with a beat that matched her own heart.

She had never seen a man without his clothing before. She opened her mouth, but did not know what to say. Cormac's smile turned somewhat sheepish. "I'll be gentle with ye, of course." He hesitated. "And if ye've changed yer mind..."

"Nay," she said quickly. "I want you. I want this. I've just never...seen a man..." Her speech faltered, and a blush heated through her.

He nodded, evidently expecting such a response, and stepped closer. "I'm hard where ye're soft." He ran his hand over his length, then shifted to brush his fingers between her thighs where her core still quivered from the force of her release. "We're made to fit together, ye and I."

She gazed up at him and tentatively reached for the unfamiliar bit of male flesh. He watched her as her fingertips explored him.

The skin was exquisitely smooth, like hot silk. But beneath, he was hard as stone, all except the tip, which was spongy and made him hiss in a breath as she explored. His muscles were tense as she stroked his length, and she considered the ways he had thus far brought her pleasure.

Gauging his reaction, she squeezed lightly. An exhale shuttered from between his teeth. Aye, he liked it. The same as she had enjoyed his ministrations.

Encouraged, she leaned forward, keeping her stare on him and extended her tongue to lick the swollen tip delicately.

CORMAC STIFFENED AT THE TOUCH OF ISOLDE'S TONGUE TO HIS prick.

She immediately backed away. "Do you not like it?"

Cormac opened his mouth, but only a little croak uttered out.

"Have I hurt you?" she gasped.

He shook his head.

The fear on her face melted into a coquettish smile. "You liked it?"

He cleared his inoperative throat. "I dinna expect..."

"I enjoyed what you did to me." A pretty blush crept over her cheeks. "I want to please you too."

She leaned forward once more and looked up at him. He dragged in a slow breath and nodded.

Her small tongue flicked out over the tip of his cock once more. His ballocks tightened at the sweet pleasure. *God's teeth.*

She licked the underside next, tracing him up from the root.

He made a fist with his hand and squeezed to maintain control. "Ye can suck it," he offered. Realizing how foolish the instruction sounded, he added, "if ye like."

She gave him a wicked little grin and parted her lips over him. Her warm breath bathed over his impossibly sensitive skin before she drew him into her hot mouth and suckled.

It was too much. If she did much more, he would lose his seed right then.

"Stop," he groaned, pulling himself free of her sensual mouth.

"Have I done it wrong?" She bit her lower lip.

He wanted to pull that lower lip free and slide his cock back into the hot, sweet temptation of her mouth. "Ye did it exactly right. Too good." He shook his head, unable to put the thoughts together to explain himself properly. "I want ye."

She took his hand and lay back on the bed, pulling him with her. Her breasts rose high and round on her chest. A bruise showed like a shadow on her ribs. Not as dark as the one on her arm, but enough to make him move with extreme care over the top of her, lest her injuries were greater than she let on.

She spread her legs to cradle his pelvis against hers, her center open for him, pink and glistening with evidence of her desire. He braced himself over her with one arm and used his free hand to guide his prick toward her damp center. She arched her hips upward with desperate eagerness.

But while he had never lain with a virgin before, he knew the first time brought some pain. Loathing the thought of hurting her, he nudged the very tip of himself inside her and hesitated.

Isolde sighed with longing. "Aye."

"It may hurt," he cautioned.

"It couldn't possibly." She writhed under him. "Not when everything feels so good."

He eased deeper in, pushing against the resistance of her tightness, having to use more effort than he wanted. Even the scant inch of him within her was enough to make his body tremble. Everything in him demanded he shove inside her and take her.

But he wouldn't. He couldn't. Not at the cost of her discomfort.

He released his prick and braced himself on the other side of her, framing his arms over her while every muscle in his body shook with forced control.

"Please." She whimpered with impatience. "Do it now. I can withstand pain."

"I dinna want to hurt ye," he gritted through his teeth.

Suddenly, she swept her leg over him, and he found himself flopped onto his back with her straddled atop him. "You won't hurt me," she assured him. Then she held him by the root, so his erection jutted straight up, aimed at her center, and penetrated herself with him.

Her eyes went wide, and her mouth opened in a startled gasp.

They both froze, him in a mix of horror and at the exquisite grip of her tight sheath. Her, most likely in surprise at the pain.

She shifted atop him. The slight wriggle of her hips against his made a fresh wave of bliss wash over him.

She drew a shaky breath. "I don't know what to do."

He put his hands to her hips and rocked her forward as he flexed his pelvis up. Her brows furrowed. He repeated this move several more times, slow and careful until the intense concentration on her face changed with the flutter of her lashes. Her brow smoothed, and her lips parted.

She followed the rhythm without having his hands guide her, rolling against his body. Her discomfort had impeded his enjoyment. Now, however, knowing she took pleasure in their union, he was free to revel in the mating of their bodies.

"Put yer hands on my chest," he instructed.

She did as he instructed and leaned forward, shifting her hips over him. He thrust into her, matching his pace with hers as her sex gripped him and squeezed with each meeting. Her breasts bounced in time with their rhythm, her small pink nipples hard and tempting him to suck them into his mouth. He cupped his hands around her bosom, thumbing the little buds as the weight of her bosom jiggled in his palms.

Isolde moved faster, and he matched her pace, both of them in a desperate frenzy of pushing, squeezing, thrusting, gripping, everything growing hotter and tighter until she threw her head back with a screaming cry. Her fingers clenched at his chest, and her sheath spasmed around his shaft, milking him toward his own release.

His climax took him hard, crashing over him and drowning him beneath a sea of euphoria that drew on for an eternity. Isolde bent forward and collapsed on his chest while the final waves of his crises lapped over him, and he became aware of their heartbeats pounding frantically against one another. He curled his arms around her and held her while their bodies cooled.

"I dinna want to hurt ye," he whispered.

"*You* didn't," she replied.

It was at that moment he realized her switching their positions wasn't due to impatience on her part. She didn't want him to have the responsibility of having caused her pain.

She pushed up and regarded him through a curtain of tousled auburn hair. Her eyes were still heavy-lidded with pleasure, her smile languid, her cheeks flushed. She pressed a kiss to his lips, bringing with her the sensual scent of roses and intimacy.

Was he in love?

Absolutely.

It was why he would do what was necessary the following day. Even if he knew it would be unforgivable.

✺ 14 ✺

I solde had never experienced such a solid night of sleep as she had snuggled in the warm comfort of Cormac's embrace. Wakefulness tugged at her, beckoning her slowly into aware-ness. A chill graced her skin, and she nudged backward toward the heat of Cormac's body. And met nothing.

She rolled over and found the bed empty.

Her heart sank with disappointment. He'd been worried that someone might view him coming to her rooms, and he was no doubt also concerned about who might see him leave. Not that it mattered as they would be wed that eve. After...

Isolde flinched with the realization of exactly what day it was and what awaited them. Edmund the Braw. A man undefeated in combat.

Fear quivered in her chest, a fear she would not allow herself to fall victim to. She had no choice but to fight Edmund, and she would never allow Cormac to stand in her place. Resolute and determined to prepare, she rose from the bed, drew on her robe to hide her nakedness and opened the door. Matilda sat beside a fire with a bit of mending in her hand.

The shutters were open, and the full morning sun shone in.

Isolde was hit with a jolt of alarm. How could it be so late in the morning already? She was due in the practice field.

"Why did you not wake me, Matilda?" Isolde asked. "We must hurry, or I will be late."

Matilda did not move but instead bent her head more determinedly over her sewing.

Something was amiss.

Ice frosted in Isolde's veins. "Where is Cormac?" She cast a glance around the room. "Where is my armor?"

At last, Matilda looked up, her face creased with guilt. "Forgive me, my lady."

"What have you done?" Isolde demanded.

Matilda shook her head as tears welled in her eyes. "If I didn't do this, you would die."

"Where is he? Where is Cormac? Matilda, what have you done?" Isolde's voice pitched with rage and frustration and grief. Because she knew where Cormac was before Matilda could answer.

"He's at the practice field, my lady," Matilda said sorrowfully.

"Where is my armor?" Isolde ordered. "Get it for me posthaste."

Again, Matilda shook her head as tears streamed down her face. "I cannot, my lady. Your armor has been relocated to Sutherland's tent."

Isolde stared at her maid in complete horror.

Matilda drew in a shaking inhale. "If you wish to attend, I've been told you may do so only as yourself, wearing one of your gowns."

A sob wrenched from the depths of Isolde's soul, a piteous, raw wail of pain.

Matilda rushed to her side. "Forgive me, my lady."

Isolde spun on her maid. "You have betrayed me most heinously."

Matilda erupted into noisy tears. "Forgive me, my lady. I could not bear the thought of your death."

"And so, you have sent the man I am to marry to his death instead." She stared with incredulity at the woman she had trusted most in the world. "There can never be forgiveness for this act."

Matilda hiccupped through her tears and nodded with an understanding that pricked at Isolde.

"He is at the practice field now?" Isolde asked.

Matilda nodded and swiped at her tears with a handkerchief. "Would you like me to dress you, my lady?" She indicated a kirtle she had already laid out. It was a simple design of pale blue linen. One that could be put on quickly. No doubt Matilda had selected it for that reason.

Guilt pinched at Isolde for her ire. "I know you did this to protect me. But you must know what it's done to my heart."

Again, Matilda nodded and set to work dressing Isolde. Though the maid's hands shook, her movements were swift as she laced Isolde into the simple kirtle and bound her long hair back in a single braid.

When she was done, Matilda stood before Isolde with her head bowed. "I only sought to protect you."

Isolde took Matilda's hot hand in hers and squeezed. "I know. Forgive me for my anger. I can't..." Her words choked off. "I can't lose him." She closed her eyes, and a tear slid down her cheek. "I'm so frightened."

It had been years since Isolde had said such words. She hated the helplessness and fear that she'd sworn she would never allow herself to feel again.

Isolde blinked her eyes open. "Stay at my side?"

Matilda tightened her hand around Isolde's. "Always, my lady."

Together, they left the room and quickly wound their way down to the practice field. A small cluster of men had already gathered, and Isolde knew the fight would begin anon. If it had not already.

Her pulse pounded like a war drum in her ears. She quickened her pace, practically running toward the group of men. Pip raced to her, but she did not stop to pet him. She didn't pause to see if Matilda followed, or bothered to care who might notice her eagerness to see Cormac. She didn't stop until she caught sight of the two men in full armor as they circled one another.

"Cease this at once," she cried as loud as she could. Beside her, Pip whimpered.

Both men paused.

Isolde found Brodie in the crowd. "I beg of you not to do this."

He sneered at her. "I see yer brother dinna bother to show up for the fight. He sent another man in his place."

"I do not love you," Isolde said vehemently. "I never will."

Brodie laughed. "It was never yer heart I was after, ye silly chit."

"I will not marry you." Isolde lifted her chin. "No man could force me to wed the likes of you. This battle is pointless."

He narrowed his eyes. "Ye will."

"I'm already wed," she said hastily. "Last night. To the Chieftain of the Sutherland clan."

Brodie cast his attention to the two warriors facing one another. "Ye mean the man my champion fights now?"

"Aye." Isolde leveled her stare at Brodie. "Wedded and bedded. You cannot have me."

Aye, it was a partial lie, but who could refute her claim?

She had won. Again.

"Call off the fight," she said. "You have already lost."

Brodie pursed his lips and casually scratched at his neck. "I dinna think so."

"How can you—?"

"Any child ye bear in the first year of our union, I'll put to death with my own sword," Brodie growled. "I willna have another man's bastard as my bairn."

"I'm already wed," Isolde protested through numb lips.

"And ye'll be a widow soon." He looked to the taller of the two warriors, most assuredly Edmund the Braw. "This fight will be to the death."

⚜

CORMAC TIGHTENED HIS GIP ON THE HILT OF HIS SWORD AS Isolde cried out in protest. He forced her from his mind and instead eyed the taller, larger warrior in front of him. One of them would not live to see midday. And it would not be Cormac.

Edmund charged with his sword arcing down. Cormac ducked right to avoid the blow. Though he missed the worst of the strike, the weapon still glanced off his side, the blade skittering over his chainmail. The force knocked the wind from Cormac's lungs, and he staggered back to recover.

Even with only a partial hit, the blow had been powerful. The battle would be difficult.

But not impossible.

Cormac had no choice but to win.

Edmund roared with bestial rage and lifted his weapon once more. Cormac leapt back to avoid the swipe of the blade and rushed forward, thrusting his own weapon at his opponent. It struck Edmund in the gut. It wouldn't slice through his chainmail, of course, but the tip would nick the skin, and the might of the strike would have an impact.

Edmund grunted and turned his sword, so the massive pommel of his hilt hurtled toward Cormac. But Cormac was faster. He ducked and rolled beneath Edmund's legs, popping up on the other side. Using his own pommel, he delivered several hard strikes to the other man's lower back.

Edmund stumbled forward and spun around, his blade

whistling through the air. If Cormac had only hit Edmund once in the back, he might have been able to avoid the path of the weapon. That second strike had cost him precious seconds.

He would need to be more prudent with his decisions, or he'd pay with his life.

Edmund's sword slammed into his arm with an impact that sent Cormac flying sideways.

His world spun for a moment before righting itself as he realized he lay on the ground. The entire left side of his body blazed with agony. Mayhap the hit had broken his arm. If so, he was grateful it had not been his dominant side.

Isolde's scream cut through the fog of pain and left him scrambling to his feet as yet another blow fell upon him. The pommel of Edmund's sword crashed into Cormac's helm, making a metallic clang echo in his ears. Cormac stumbled backward and swung his own weapon at his opponent. This time, he struck Edmund in the thigh with full force.

Edmund issued a howl of rage and limped backward. Cormac took advantage of the injury and caught Edmund's good leg just behind the knee, sending the other man crashing to the ground. Edmund fell hard enough to knock his head back, and his helm tumbled off. The massive warrior blinked in surprise at the brilliant sky above.

Cormac pushed his blade against Edmund's tender neck. Before Cormac could drive the point of his sword into his opponent, Edmund rolled away and leapt to his feet. He ran forward, and his entire body weight slammed into Cormac, sending them both to the ground.

The hilt in Cormac's hand was knocked free and sent his blade tumbling out of reach. He was unarmed. But the fight was not yet over. He struck out at Edmund with his metal fists, landing a punch on the other man's naked face.

Edmund shoved his knee into Cormac's injured arm. Stars blazed in hot agony before Cormac's eyes, stunning him momentarily. A powerful hit slammed into Cormac's chin, and sunlight dazzled his vision.

Without his helm, he would be vulnerable for a death blow. The same as Edmund had been.

Quick as lightning, Cormac rolled away, knowing his opponent would use the opportunity to bring his sword down. No sooner had the thought entered Cormac's mind, Edmund's blade came down once more, this time striking Cormac's chest only an inch away from his exposed neck. Pain exploded in the place Edmund had struck, but Cormac was still alive. Edmund raised his weapon, preparing to strike again until Cormac was dead.

But Cormac was not done fighting. He pushed aside the pain. He rolled and he rolled and he rolled, evading Edmund's blade as he ended up where his own weapon had fallen.

The world spun, but the clink of steel that met his gauntlet told Cormac he'd found his sword. At the moment he paused, Edmund rose over him, readying the blade to plunge down once more.

However, before Edmund could strike, Cormac punched his blade into the air and caught Edmund at the hollow of his throat. The razor-sharp blade slid with ease through sinewy tendon and bone and soft flesh alike. Blood gushed from the wound and splashed over Cormac, but he didn't stop until Edmund's blade slipped from his grasp, and he collapsed to the ground.

Only then did Cormac get to his feet and pull the blade from Edmund's fatal injury. The large warrior's eyes blinked once in surprise as a gurgle sounded from the gaping wound at his throat. Cormac stared down at his dying opponent.

His head spun with the effects of having been struck by a pommel and kicked in the chin, and his heartbeat was discernible with a painful pulse in his arm.

But he had done it. He had won. He was still alive.

And Isolde was his.

He threw his bloody sword to the grass beside Edmund and glared up at Brodie. "Get away from my wife."

Wife.

The word was new and wonderful on his tongue. He'd heard Isolde's claim that they were already wed and was eager for nightfall to come so they could meet with the priest and truly make it so.

He strode toward Brodie. "If I ever see ye near her again, I'll kill ye too."

Brodie's gaze was fixed on his now-dead champion, his gaze fierce before meeting Cormac's eyes. "Ye'll pay for this, Sutherland," Brodie hissed. "Ye'll pay."

"I think ye should leave." Lachlan edged in front of Brodie and put his hand to his hilt.

"He won fairly." Duncan appeared beside him and followed suit.

Isolde ran to Cormac and threw her arms around him, almost knocking him backward. By some miracle, he managed to stay upright despite his injuries and held her to him, drawing in her sweet, familiar rose scent.

There had been a brief moment when he'd feared never to have the opportunity to do this again.

But he had won.

"You should never have kept me from this fight," Isolde said in a trembling voice. "You could have been killed."

"I wasna." He hugged her against him with his good arm.

He'd been at risk of being killed, aye, but he knew without a shadow of a doubt that she would have been slain. Her body could never have sustained the blows that his had.

If she had fought that day, she would be dead.

Brodie was forced to leave the practice field. His brothers went with him, but they left the body of their champion behind. No doubt their servants would be by at some point to clear it away.

For his part, Cormac kept his gaze away from the man he had killed. He hadn't wanted to take Edmund's life. He hadn't wanted any of this. But he would do it all again to keep Isolde safe.

With his uninjured arm still around her, Cormac allowed Isolde to lead him toward his tent. His body was battered, his head still spun with the hits to his skull, his chest ached where the blade had come down with force upon it and his heart was heavy for the life he'd taken.

But Isolde was safe. Tonight, they would be wed, and Cormac's people would have the food they needed to survive.

For the first time in far too long, everything was going exactly right for Cormac.

I solde had thought she would lose Cormac that day. And while she was elated at his victory, she could not help but notice how he leaned heavily upon her as they walked to his tent. She'd wanted him to come to the castle, but he refused, saying he would not do so until they were wed.

He was a stubborn man.

A stubborn, wonderful man that had captured her heart in the most uncommon way.

Cormac staggered slightly, almost falling on poor Pip, who had refused to leave her side. Isolde tried to grab Cormac's arm to hold him to her when he grunted in pain and pitched forward. Isolde gasped in alarm, but before he could hit the ground, Alan was there, groaning with the effort of keeping the much larger man upright.

"Cormac," Isolde cried out.

He groaned. "I need to lay down."

"Can you walk?" She asked. "We're nearly to your tent."

"Of course I can," he replied resolutely from against a sagging Alan.

She pulled at Cormac's other arm as he slowly straightened.

He huffed a breath, stiffened his back and strode to the tent without assistance, his face a mask of sheer determination.

A stubborn man indeed.

But Isolde was glad for it. Most likely, that stubbornness was what had kept him alive.

Once they were in the tent, Matilda set to gathering fresh garments for Cormac. Alan and Isolde helped remove Cormac's chainmail and gambeson, as well as the thin linen beneath, to ensure he had no critical injuries. Pip lay by the tent flap, his anxious gaze fixed on Isolde.

"Does anything hurt?" she asked.

Cormac laughed. Then winced. "Dinna trouble yerself. I'll be fine."

A massive bruise showed red black on his upper left arm. She had noticed him favoring it earlier, and it was the one she had grabbed when he stumbled earlier. The pain of the injury was most likely what had caused him to fall.

"Move your arm," Isolde said.

Cormac ground his teeth and rolled his shoulder with a grimace.

Isolde nodded. "Now bend it at the elbow."

He complied, his mouth set in a tight line.

Isolde breathed a sigh of relief. "I don't believe it to be broken." She'd seen a break once before where the white of the bone had jutted from the knight's elbow as he screamed in agony. He had not been able to move his arm at all.

Still, it was best to be assured of his health, and so Matilda was tasked with locating a healer. An older woman came to the tent, smelling of herbs and smoke. She searched over his body with her withered hands while Matilda and Alan waited outside. Once done, the woman announced Cormac's injuries, with time, would heal and cause no further damage. She did stress his need for rest. Not that Isolde expected him to listen to such advice.

"Let us leave," Cormac said when the healer had gone.

"Now?" Isolde gazed up at him. She couldn't stop staring at him, as if having to confirm to herself repeatedly that he was alive and well.

If he wished to leave at that very moment, she would abandon everything behind to follow him.

He stroked her cheek with the back of his knuckle and stared down at her with matched intensity. "On the morrow. After we've wed. I dinna want anyone to question our union. We can return to Scotland and ye can inform yer brother of our marriage by missive."

Isolde nodded and squeezed his hand. The melee would be the following day, but she had no interest in staying to observe the mock battle. "I should like that very much," she replied. "I'll return to the castle with Matilda to have my chambers packed for our departure."

"And I'll find Graham to let him know we'll be returning earlier than anticipated."

Cormac pulled Isolde to his side with his healthy arm, his movements gentle in light of both their injuries. "I enjoyed calling ye 'wife' earlier. I look forward to calling ye 'wife' henceforth." He pressed his mouth to hers in a tender kiss.

Isolde wanted to remain locked in the warmth of his arms, kissing his sensual lips, and reassuring herself again and again that he was still alive and that he was hers. However, she had much to prepare for their departure.

"There's only one final thing I need."

Cormac gave her a suggestive grin. "And what is that?"

She returned his grin with a coquettish one. "My armor."

CORMAC APPROACHED THE OUTSKIRTS OF THE VILLAGE WHERE he had promised to meet Isolde. His stomach twisted with apprehension.

She would not be pleased with what he had to tell her. He had gone to Graham to explain his early departure and discovered the Rosses had given his brother no choice but to fight against them. He had, of course, anticipated Cormac would join him.

Cormac didn't protest. Not when he knew his brother needed him. They never let one another down.

While he was anticipating making Isolde his wife, he was not looking forward to telling Isolde of his plans. She would be upset, especially in light of his injuries.

In truth, he was much better now. The blow to his arm had merely bruised it deeply, but nothing was broken. The injuries to his head had not addled him as thoroughly as he had initially feared.

Suddenly Isolde was there, sauntering torward him and all thoughts of telling her about the melee the following day slipped away. She was awash in the moonlight, wearing a lovely blue kirtle with small beads that winked like stars in the semi-darkness. Matilda was at her side, ready to bear witness to their union, the same as Alan, who followed behind Cormac. Graham had wanted to come but had to see about his own lady

Pip raced toward her with his usual eagerness, excitedly greeting her before Cormac even had a chance. Isolde stood as he approached and smiled at him so broadly and beautifully that his heart squeezed.

She wore a crown of white flowers on her head, her long auburn hair left unbound to blow gently around her in the light breeze. She reached for him as he approached, and he caught her slender hand in his, lifting it to his lips. No longer caring if he looked like a courtier or not. He simply wanted nothing more than her happiness.

Mayhap it would be best to tell her about the melee after they wed. Aye, that's what he would do. Wait until they were alone and could speak privately.

"Will ye marry me now, my bonny Isolde?" he asked.

"Aye." She pushed their clasped hands to her chest. "With all the joy in my heart."

Together, their small party entered the village to where the priest awaited them in the small stone church. They made their vows there, amid several rows of empty pews and whitewash chipping from every corner of the stone walls. Only several candles had been lit, giving off more greasy smoke than light. It was not the typical wedding of an earl's daughter, let alone that of a chieftain.

But the woman he married was what made it all perfect.

In the end, the priest pronounced them man and wife in God's eyes and those of man. They kissed chastely, and with that, their souls were bound for all eternity.

They intended to stay the night in the castle, without fear of reproach, in light of their marriage. Their party returned to the Rose Citadel together, with Isolde and Cormac in front and Pip bouncing excitedly back and forth between Isolde and Alan.

Cormac kept Isolde tucked close to him on his good side. This was yet another opportunity that would be perfect for him to confess that he had to fight in the melee the following day. He was in the midst of composing what he meant to say when Isolde spoke.

"Tell me about Sutherland." She smiled up at him. "I want to learn more about my new home."

It pleased him that she was so eager to learn of the land where she would be living alongside him, ruling his people. He meant only to tell her of the castle, and several of the servants who would be there for whatever task she needed. But the sparkle in her eyes was so bright and her expression so eager that he found himself going into great detail on the beauty of the land: the emerald-green hills dotted with patches of purple heather and a rich blue sky sprawling endlessly overhead with clouds spread about like tufts of cotton.

"I'm eager to go," she said.

"As am I. Speaking of it has made me realize how much I miss home." He led her up the stairs of the Rose Citadel to the guest suites where her rooms were located. Their journey had been quicker than he had anticipated. Once more, he had squandered his opportunity to tell her about the melee.

The main room to her apartment had two carefully packed trunks set to the side. Isolde indicated the trunks. "I'm quite obviously ready for an early morning departure."

Cormac winced as she pulled him toward the private bedchamber they would share once more. She immediately let go of his hand. "What is it?"

He led her into the chamber, closing the door and latching it behind him. "I canna leave on the morrow."

She blinked. "Why not?"

He sighed and ran a hand through his hair. "Graham must participate in the melee tomorrow, and I promised I would fight at his side. As we've always done."

She shook her head. "You can't. You're injured."

"I've had worse." He winked at her.

"Not before a fight, surely." Her eyes welled with tears. "I feared I would lose you forever today. I cannot stand the thought that you would put your life at risk once more. Especially when your body has not fully recovered."

"It willna be as dangerous." He took her hand in his and turned her forearm over to reveal the dark bruise on her fair skin. He ran his thumb gently over it. "Ye're as stubborn as I am when it comes to what ye know ye have to see to. Isolde, I must do this."

She nodded solemnly. She understood as he knew she would. He didn't like it any more than she did, but he could not leave his brother to defend himself in the melee.

They kissed then, a hungry, desperate kiss that spoke of their concern for one another, for all the feelings words could never adequately convey. And later, when they joined together, they took their time loving each other. They learned each other's bodies, pleasing one another until their skin was slick with sweat and their limbs trembled with exhaustion. They cherished the night before the next day's fight, not stopping until they fell into a languid sleep.

For the following day would be another battle. Brodie's visage flashed in Cormac's mind just before sleep claimed him: the twisted mask of rage.

Cormac would do well to mind his enemy, for surely Brodie would come seeking vengeance.

❧ 16 ☙

The following morning, Isolde woke to Cormac sleeping next to her. No longer was this the day they journeyed to Sutherland. This would be the day of the melee, with Cormac once more placed in danger.

Only this time, she had a plan at the ready.

They took their time rousing; their bodies loathe to pull away from one another. Yet as he rose from the bed, the heat of his skin against hers was lost. Protests circled in her mind regardless of how many times she shoved them away.

"I wish you would not go." Isolde settled her feet on the cool wooden floors and drew herself upright from the bed as well.

"I'd prefer to be leaving for Sutherland instead." Cormac belted his hose and drew his tunic over his head. "And we will. On the morrow."

He crossed the room to stand before her and opened his powerful arms. She allowed him to pull her against the heat of his strong chest, where the steady beat of his heart ticked its rhythm against her cheek. How she wished she could stay like that forever, locked in the comfort of his embrace.

"Be safe, husband." She rose on her tiptoes and pressed a kiss to his mouth.

"With ye to come back to, wife, no' even heaven itself could stop me from returning." He smoothed a hand over her hair and cupped her face.

It wasn't heaven she worried about. It was the Rosses. Particularly Brodie Ross, who had proven to be an adversary that did not readily admit defeat. "Who is it Graham seeks to fight against in the melee?" Isolde asked.

Cormac hesitated long enough for her to know the answer before he replied. "One of Brodie's brothers."

As she had anticipated. She nodded. "Do not underestimate him."

"Dinna worry after me." Cormac kissed her. The brush of their lips was quick but still intimate. It made her want to keep him there for all eternity.

"I can't help it," Isolde said in a pained voice.

"I'll return posthaste." With one final kiss, he was gone, leaving the castle for his tent where Alan would help dress him in his armor.

As soon as Cormac departed, Isolde found Matilda in the main room by the fire as she worked on the mending. "I require your assistance," Isolde said.

Matilda practically threw her sewing to the floor and flew to her feet. "Of course, my lady. Anything."

"Prepare me for the melee." Isolde leveled her gaze at her maid. "As my brother."

Matilda's brows drew together with concern.

"I am going to ensure Cormac remains safe," Isolde explained. "He sustained injuries yesterday. I only want to reassure myself no harm will come to him."

Matilda's shoulders relaxed from their tense perch, and she quickly rushed to do as Isolde bid. First, she bound Isolde's hair back in a thick braid, then put on the gambeson and hose, followed by the chainmail and surcoat. Once done, Isolde dropped the helm over her head. She suppressed a shudder at her limited visibility and how vividly it reminded her of the fight with Brodie.

Cormac had been correct when he'd said she would have died against Edmund. After witnessing the blows Cormac had endured, Isolde knew she would have been incapacitated after the first one.

She would not have walked away from that fight. Cormac had kept her safe, as he'd promised he would the day he'd made the vow to protect her.

Now, as his wife, she would do the same for him.

She waited until the first charge on horseback was over and several knights had descended into hand-to-hand combat before joining the field on foot. She needed to be as close to the warriors as she could get, and horseback wouldn't allow that. After all, she wasn't there to win. She was there to protect.

Several knights attacked her as soon as she entered the field. One came at her from the right, but she blocked his blow and managed to evade the thrust of his pike as someone else locked him in combat from the other side. Another came at her head-on, swinging his iron-spiked club.

These were lethal weapons being used in a melee that was supposed to be absent death.

She shifted her horse away from the attack as the knight strode off toward another hapless victim. A band of tall men with red-and-white surcoats traveling in a group together caught her attention. She recognized their surcoats as the Ross clan's. No doubt, the five brothers and several of their warriors. The group didn't appear to be fighting actively, so much as heading in a specific direction.

Isolde could make out the Sutherland crest on Cormac and Graham's surcoats in the distance. Which was exactly the direction that the Ross brothers were heading.

No doubt to exact revenge.

CORMAC COULD PRACTICALLY SMELL THE ODOR OF THE ROSS clan advancing toward them. They stank of weakness, failure and blind vengeance.

"They're coming," he said.

Graham nodded and hefted his bladed mace. Lachlan and Duncan did likewise with their pikes. They'd all left their swords back at the tent, knowing the men who would attack them would be using weapons made for getting through chainmail. To do otherwise would put them at a great disadvantage.

Hoofbeats thundered as the Rosses came at them all at once, a pack of twelve roaring warriors intent on killing with war hammers and maces and skinny-speared pikes. Brodie charged at Cormac as another brother, presumably Baston, went for Graham and the others dispersed between them.

Brodie swiped his war hammer at Cormac's left arm, exactly over his injury from Edmund. Cormac managed to get his mace up in time to block the blow. Had it struck, it might have been debilitating.

Clangs and grunts echoed as Graham, Lachlan and Duncan fought the other Ross warriors in unbalanced matches.

Two more warriors joined Brodie, all coming at Cormac at the same time. He moved as swiftly as he could to block the blows, but one of Brodie's hits made it past his defenses and slammed into his back, knocking the wind from his lungs and leaving fire in its place. A second hit followed the first and Cormac rocked on his saddle, his balance shifting. The pain in his back had been so stunning, he couldn't properly catch his balance and pitched from his horse.

He gasped for breath at the hard landing and staggered backward in an attempt to regain his bearings before resuming the fight on foot. Brodie leapt from his own horse, joining Cormac on the ground, and lashing out with the heavy metal head of his weapon.

A perfectly placed blow could easily shatter one of Cormac's bones.

Another warrior charged at him, one shorter and thinner than Brodie. An easier target.

Cormac lifted his mace and brought it down hard on the warrior's shoulder. The needle-like blades of the mace sunk through the man's chain, turning it red with blood. He cried out in agony as Cormac jerked his weapon free. It gave way with a wet, sucking sound.

His opponent doubled over in pain. That was when Cormac caught sight of the person racing toward them with purpose. His heart caught as he recognized the surcoat. Dark blue with white trim and a white moon and sun.

The surcoat of the Earl of Easton.

Which meant the person charging toward the heat of battle between the Sutherlands and the Rosses was Isolde.

Cormac bellowed his disapproval; his attention so fixated on her as she neared them that he did not see the hammer come down upon him. It struck his left arm with a hit that glanced off his chainmail and left his bones rattling. His vision clouded in his agony.

Brodie took a menacing step toward Cormac and lifted the hammer with intent. The pain kept Cormac frozen in place for a half a second too long, leaving him at the momentary mercy of his enemy.

Isolde leapt from her horse, plowing her full body weight into Brodie, so he was jarred sideways. As he drew himself upright, she retrieved the pike his brother had dropped on the ground and came to Cormac's wounded side.

"Ye shouldna be here," he growled.

"I see ye've called on yer new ally's aid," Brodie said from beneath his helm. "I hadna realized Lord Easton harbored such affection for the Sutherland clan."

Brodie's injured warrior sat off to the side, gasping and completely ignored by the other warriors who still fought.

"I'll kill ye both for yer betrayal." Brodie readjusted the hammer in his hand as one of the men fighting Graham turned away from him and toward Cormac.

"I dinna want ye here," Cormac said to Isolde. "Go now."

"Nay." She hefted the pike in front of her.

"Get Lord Easton away from Sutherland," Brodie said in a harsh cry as he charged at them.

Suddenly, another warrior was on them as well. Cormac's arm did not appear to be broken, but neither could he adequately use it, leaving him to swing his mace with only the strength of one arm rather than two. It was a disadvantage that could cost them their lives.

Much as he tried to stop it from happening, Brodie managed to shove him back with rapid, repeated arcs of his war hammer. In doing so, Cormac and Isolde were separated.

Exactly as Brodie had wanted.

One of the brothers swung his hammer at her, catching her in the head and knocking her forcefully to the ground. She did not rise.

"Nay," Cormac howled.

The two men battling her turned their attention on him. One, he managed to strike with his mace, but not before Brodie could heft Isolde to her feet and race off with her light frame slung over his back.

Cormac bellowed in rage, his body exploding with energy as he struck at his opponent again and again and again. He didn't stop until the heavy head of the mace sank into the softness of a chainmail-covered body. The Ross warrior in front of him sank to his knees.

Cormac did not wait to see if the man got back up, or for the other man to attack once more. Nay, he sprinted across the field as fast as his chainmail and thick gambeson would allow, heading in the direction he'd seen Brodie take Isolde. He found Brodie on a horse with Isolde's limp body secured between his arms, racing away.

Frantic, Cormac scanned the area for his horse, unable to find him after having been unhorsed. A lone black destrier stood beside an unmoving knight. Cormac leapt onto the horse and snapped its reins, guiding the beast to follow Brodie.

No matter what it took, Cormac would rescue his wife.

17

Pain echoed in Isolde's temples. It rang in her ears with an intensity that slowly brought her to awareness. Darkness surrounded her, and her breath huffed raggedly in her own ears. She shook her head, but the sensation didn't clear.

Her helm. She still was wearing her helm.

"Why did ye decide to go back on our plan?" Rough hands hauled her upright, and Brodie's face came into the view of her visor. "We had an arrangement. I'd already set my men into action against yer cursed king. And now ye've deprived me of yer sister's dowry?"

Isolde's head lolled slightly, and a hollow ache resonated in time with her pulse. She smirked at his reference to her dowry. That was all he had ever wanted. That was all any man had ever wanted.

Except for Cormac.

She glanced around the surrounding area. Was he nearby? Had he been injured?

She saw no one else around them. There were naught but green, open fields, several trees and a nearby hill.

"Are ye even listening to me?" He shoved his meaty hand

against her chin, knocking her helm away and unveiling a bright sun.

She squinted against the brilliance as her eyes adjusted, revealing Brodie's wide-eyed shock.

He stared at her, his mouth hanging open. "Lady Isolde?"

Senses now returned, she shoved away from him. "Unhand me, you cur."

"Was it ye?" He asked incredulously.

The fresh air swept against her cheeks like heaven but brought the ache in her head to life once more. She winced and took in the small copse of trees nearby. If she could escape into them, she might be able to hide.

They were not far off from the melee, which was discernible by the clashing weapons and shouts of men. She could run toward the melee as well if she was free.

She need only be faster than Brodie.

"Aye." She glared at him without bothering to hide her disgust and rage. "All this time, it was me. The one who issued the challenge when my brother was too much of a coward to so do. And the one who beat you."

Brodie scoffed. "I dinna believe ye. No way could a lass be strong enough to beat me in a fight."

"I didn't say I was stronger than you." Isolde lifted her chin up and met his gaze with defiance. "But I was far cleverer and much faster."

Brodie smacked the back of his hand across her face with a force that made her head snap to the side. Pain exploded where his gauntlet met with the exposed skin of her cheek.

"Why did ye side with Sutherland?" Brodie demanded.

Sutherland.

Cormac.

No doubt he was still on the field, locked in combat against an unfair number of men.

Isolde didn't bother answering. She owed Brodie no explanation. A horse was several paces behind her. If she could get to it, she knew she was swift enough to sweep onto its back and ride away.

Enraged, Brodie grabbed her by the neck of her surcoat and held her several inches in the air. "I asked why. I demand an answer."

"Because he sees me for more than my wealth and noble birth." Isolde twisted out of Brodie's grasp and stumbled as her feet met the ground once more. "He respects me for the woman I am and for the strength he knows I possess. He's an honorable man. The kind of man you'll never be."

Isolde had anticipated her words would anger Brodie. She had not, however, expected his laughter.

He shook his head. "Ye stupid chit. Do ye have any idea how much ye've been fooled?"

Isolde glared at him. "The only fool here is you if you expect to turn me against my husband."

The horse was nearly at her back. Two more steps and she could mount it and ride off. She edged nearer to the beast, putting herself closer to the opportunity for escape.

Brodie glanced behind her at the horse and grabbed her surcoat, jerking her away from her one opportunity for freedom. "Ye consider yerself cleverer than I, but I'm no' an idiot."

He shoved Isolde to the ground. "The man ye claim loves ye without any of yer dowry approached me this past winter seeking aid to feed his clan."

Isolde didn't bother replying. She knew what Brodie was trying to do and she wouldn't fall prey.

"Ye dinna believe me." Brodie lifted his shoulders and a casual shrug. "It doesna matter—ye'll find out for yerself if ye ever get to see his clan. If he lives that long. They dinna even have enough food to feed their people."

Isolde narrowed her eyes at him. What he said was ridiculous.

Why then did an uncertain twinge knot in her stomach?

"What do you intend to do with me?" Isolde demanded.

"I was going to hold ye for ransom." A slow grin spread over Brodie's face. "But now, I think I'll return ye to yer brother and let ye confess what ye've done. In the meantime, I'll ensure ye become a widow, so ye are free to follow through on your brother's contract that we wed."

In the distance, a rider approached on a black steed. Not just any rider. One wearing a red-and-yellow surcoat with stars.

Cormac.

Her heartbeat quickened. He'd come for her.

She kept her stare purposefully locked on Brodie to ensure she didn't alert him to Cormac's presence.

"I'll refuse to marry you," Isolde swore.

Brodie rolled his eyes, his patience evidently at its end. "Ye willna have a choice. Yer brother will force—" He paused, evidently listening intently and glanced behind him.

Before Isolde suspected what he might do, Brodie yanked her back against him and put a blade to her throat. "I'll kill her rather than allow ye to take her."

Cormac approached and drew to a stop several feet away. He ripped off his helm, his eyes wild. "If ye harm her, I'll no' rest until every member of yer family is slain."

"Tell her, Sutherland," Brodie said. "Tell her how ye wed her for her dowry."

Isolde's heart caught in her chest.

"Release my wife," Cormac growled.

"Confess," Brodie barked harshly.

"This isna any of yer concern." Cormac looked to Isolde, his features drawn tight.

Brodie chuckled cruelly. "Because ye dinna want to confess the truth of it. How yer people have no food and are starving. How ye'd do anything to get it for them, even steal a betrothed lass from another man."

This time, Cormac didn't reply.

Isolde's head ached, and her mind spun. "Cormac...tell him that isn't true."

Cormac's gaze lowered. Guilty. He looked guilty.

Isolde's chest squeezed painfully.

It couldn't be true.

Could it?

"That was before I knew ye," Cormac said. "Before I realized—"

"She's heard enough." Brodie pulled her backward with him toward the horse. "I'll be returning her to her brother."

She didn't fight Brodie this time, not when she was so numb. And what did it matter? At least Brodie had been honest about his intentions with her.

Tears burned in her eyes, and emotion knotted hard at the back of her throat.

Cormac had sought her out for her dowry. He had used her, just like every other man tried to. Only he had lied to her about it and made her think he saw her as more than a dowry.

She had believed him, and he had offered her a feigned love. She had been the greatest of fools. And now she would pay a steep price.

જ⁂ૐ

CORMAC WAS LOSING ISOLDE. NOT JUST TO BRODIE, WHO WAS dragging her away with a blade at her neck, but by the tears streaming down her face. Cormac's arm ached from where Brodie had struck him, but it was nothing compared to the agony of her thinking he'd betrayed her.

He couldn't lose her. Not like this. He'd just as soon allow his heart to be cut from his chest than have his wife dragged away from him in such a manner.

"Remove yer hands from my wife," Cormac bellowed from the depths of his soul.

"Ye dinna want him, do ye?" Brodie hissed into Isolde's ear.

She gritted her teeth and tears welled in her eyes with a look of such hurt that it cut him to the quick.

"I love ye, Isolde," Cormac cried.

A sob choked from her lips.

"I love ye," he repeated. "I did when I asked ye to wed me, and I do now still. I always will."

Tears streamed down her face.

"Brodie was correct when he said we dinna have enough food," Cormac said. "Blair is a lad I grew up with. He starved to death so that his wee son could live. Ines was an old woman who cared for others. She distributed her portions so quietly through the people that we dinna know what she'd been doing until the day she was found dead in her home, so skinny she weighed no more than a child." A knot formed in the back of his throat as he spoke of his people and what they had suffered. "Ewan and Gregor were two lads whose mother died early on, but they dinna want to tell anyone. They were found dead in their hut, their mouths green from the grass they'd eaten to assuage their empty bellies."

Tears blurred Cormac's vision, but he didn't care. "I have watched my people starve. I have seen my friends die. I did go to the Ross clan seeking aid. Aye, I'd do anything to save my people."

"Even marry me," Isolde choked out.

He winced. "I'm honored to marry ye, Isolde. I came here seeking yer hand for coin. Aye, Brodie's right about that. But that isna why I asked ye to marry me."

Brodie pushed the blade harder to her throat.

"I was going to walk away from ye," Cormac confessed. "I was willing to sacrifice something I knew could save my people—yer dowry—out of respect and care for ye."

"But ye dinna," Brodie sneered.

Cormac wasn't looking at his adversary anymore. His entire attention was focused on Isolde. "My brother opened my eyes to the realization that I wasn't using ye. Because it wasna yer dowry that I wanted." He leapt down from his horse. "It was *ye*."

"Dinna come any closer," Brodie warned.

"I respect ye, Isolde." Cormac ensured his right arm was obscured by his horse. "I love ye." He paused and let the impact of his words sink into his own soul. "I promised ye one thing, do ye remember?"

She nodded, and a silent tear ran down her cheek.

He'd vowed to protect her, and he would do it now. He tilted his head discreetly to the side.

Isolde gritted her teeth and knocked the blade away from her neck with her forearm as she darted away. At the same time, Cormac loosed the dagger he was holding and sent it sailing toward Brodie.

The eldest Ross brother had never been particularly dexterous, having always relied on his strength instead. It was to his detriment now. The blade sank into his neck, and a gush of blood spilled over his armor, staining the surcoat crimson.

Isolde ran to Cormac and threw herself in his arms. He cupped her chin and gently lifted it, carefully examining her tear-stained face to confirm she had not been injured.

"I love ye, Isolde," he said vehemently.

"And I love you," she replied.

Such beautiful, sweet words. He closed his eyes against the emotion of them and pulled her against his chest, favoring his injured arm. "Dinna come out to any more fights looking to save the likes of me though, aye?"

"You know I cannot promise that," Isolde said against his surcoat.

Cormac chuckled to himself and stroked his gauntlet over her hair, hating the thick leather and steel separating them. Aye, he did know that, but it didn't mean he'd ever stop asking.

"I'm sorry about your people." She lifted her head. "You should have told me."

He wiped away her tears. "Ye mean woo ye with my people's plight rather than my fine dancing?"

A smile broke over her lips. "Actually, I think it was how you complimented my breasts upon our first meeting that won my heart."

"I'll keep that in mind." He winked at her.

Her gaze slid to where Brodie lay face-down in a pool of blood on the ground. "What should we do about him?"

"It's no' uncommon for battles to extend beyond the melee lines any more than it is uncommon for men to die. He'll be found, and his family can provide a proper burial." Cormac looked to the hill where the melee went on in full force. "Let us ensure Graham is safe."

They left the knight's horse and took only Brodie's beast and rode together up the hill to survey the melee. Several more of the Ross clan had fallen while Graham, Lachlan and Duncan gained ground.

"We should go to them," Isolde said.

We.

Meaning Isolde would be back in battle once more.

Cormac frowned. "Graham is a strong warrior and flanked by Lachlan and Duncan, the remaining men can be handled. I'll send Alan in my stead. Let us leave this place and return to Sutherland."

"I should like to go first to see my brother. I ought to return his armor to him." She surveyed the melee before them. "And there is something I wish to say to him as well."

"Aye, of course." Cormac turned the horse in the direction of the castle and rode back toward the Rose Citadel with Isolde.

With most people occupied by the daily activities and the excitement of the melee, they were able to make it into the Rose Citadel without being seen by many. Not that it mattered. They would be gone within the hour.

Alan stood outside Isolde's chambers with Pip, who barreled

toward her in unhindered excitement. The dog bounced about on his forelegs in an effort to clamber up her greaves in his eagerness to greet her. Cormac didn't bother to chastise Alan for Pip's lack of training, not when laughter came from beneath Isolde's helm.

The door to Isolde's rooms opened, and Matilda exclaimed with delight to see her mistress returned.

Isolde entered her chamber and Cormac pulled Alan aside. "Gather my belongings from the tent, then prepare yerself to join Graham and the others on the battlefield. I have Brodie's horse, but Lady Sutherland will need one. Once the melee has concluded, tell my brother I will see ye both in Sutherland."

Graham knew that there was the possibility that Cormac and Isolde would leave the tournament early per their discussion the prior day. Alan had proven himself to be a skilled fighter, and Cormac knew he would ensure Graham remained safe.

"I supposed I've been helpful to ye after all, eh?" Alan scratched his jaw. "And that means you'll be needing me in Scotland too."

Cormac put a hand on the other man's shoulder. "Ye've done well, lad." He gave Alan's shoulder a light shake. "But dinna get cocky about it."

"Absolutely not." Alan's eyes twinkled. "But take Pip with you. I know my lady will treat him well, and I'll see him when I join you in Sutherland."

"He's yer dog," Cormac said.

"Aye, he is. Consider it job security." Alan grinned and departed to prepare Cormac's horse and belongings.

Cormac entered the suite of rooms and found Isolde in her bedchamber wearing only the gambeson. She broke free from Matilda, who was helping her remove her armor, and ran into his arms.

He caught her and cradled her to him, relishing the feel of her with him once more. "Thank ye for believing in me," he said earnestly.

"Thank you for explaining yourself." A shadow crossed over her eyes. "I thought...I thought you didn't...."

He put a finger to her lips to still the words from spilling from her lips and met her gaze. "I love ye, Isolde." He cupped her face in his hands. "My wife, my love."

He pressed a kiss to her brow and noticed Matilda slip from the room, drawing the door closed behind her.

"I love you, Cormac." Isolde curled her arms around his neck, and her lips found his once more.

He pulled free the ties of her gambeson, and the tip of her tongue grazed his lower lip. Desire slammed into him. He desired her, desperate to show her with every part of his body how much he loved her, worshipped her, needed her.

His heartbeat quickened as he slid her gambeson from her shoulders, revealing the thin linen beneath. A band of white binding had been wound around her breasts.

The energy from the battle still coursed through his blood, hot and ready. His prick stirred with longing as he drew off her linen sark.

She gave him a languid smile that made his cock even harder. "What are you doing?"

"Planning to show ye how much I love ye." He loosened the end of the binding around her chest and slowly unraveled the linen from around her bosom.

Her only reply was a soft moan as she melted against him and worked at the ties of his chainmail.

⚜

ISOLDE WAS NOT PLAGUED BY FEAR AS THEIR HORSES CAME TO A stop in front of Easton Castle. Her brother had come out to greet them, having no doubt been notified of their arrival by one of his soldiers. The sun cast a brilliant glint of gold that day, forcing Gilbert to squint up at her where she remained on horseback. Pip had been trotting alongside her and now gave a low growl at the earl.

Gilbert tossed the dog a sneer of disgust, then shifted his attention back to Isolde. "I hope you've come to beg my forgiveness for what you've done."

"Ye should be begging for hers," Cormac said from where he sat on his horse behind Isolde.

"I've come to return your armor." She slid off her steed and eyed her brother. Pip immediately settled protectively in front of her. "But I will offer no apologies for what I was forced to do by your cowardice."

Gilbert's mouth opened to protest, but Isolde continued speaking, "'Tis you who has greatly wronged not only me, but also our country."

His eyes narrowed. "How dare you speak to me with such impertinence?"

Cormac leapt down from his horse to stand beside Isolde. "How dare ye speak to her with such condescension after everything ye've done to her?"

The earl squinted up at Cormac. "You forget yourself, Brodie."

"I'm no' Brodie," Cormac replied.

Gilbert stepped closer and peered up at Cormac, lifting his palm to shield the glare of the sun. "All you Scotsmen look alike," he muttered. "Where is Brodie, and who is this man?"

"I'm Cormac Sutherland, Chieftain of the Sutherland clan," Cormac replied. The note of authority and confidence in his voice made Isolde's back straighten with pride. He looked at her and took her hand in his. "And husband to Lady Sutherland."

Gilbert's beady stare bounced between them, his confusion evident. "What has happened? Where is Brodie?"

"Brodie is dead," Isolde replied. "And whatever arrangement you worked out with him should be stopped and buried with him. I know exactly what you've done."

Her brother glanced around nervously. "I'm afraid I don't

know what you're speaking of. Come inside so that we might have a proper conversation."

Isolde turned her attention to the castle whose interior was as cold as her brother's affection for her. Any happiness she'd had in her life prior to Cormac had died with her mother. There was naught inside for her but disappointment and lies.

"I will never step foot in Easton Castle again," she said. "We will speak here for a moment more, and then we will be on our way."

Gilbert huffed a pout of frustration. "You don't get to—"

Cormac stepped forward and crossed his arms over his chest. "Mind how ye speak to my wife."

"You won't see a single coin of her dowry." Gilbert put his hands on his hips, his demeanor as petulant as his voice.

Pip gave a low growl and shifted his weight from one paw to the other.

"We're married." Isolde smiled at her brother sweetly. "You haven't a choice. Father put a stipulation in his will regarding my dowry— it goes to my husband without question."

Gilbert's lips pinched together. He knew well there was little ability to protest on his part. He could delay, of course, but given the fearful stares he cast up at Cormac, Isolde did not think it likely. Especially when her brother lacked a steel spine.

"I'd like my armor back," Gilbert demanded.

"Of course," Isolde agreed. "In exchange for my belongings that you so considerately had packed in my time away."

Gilbert glowered. "Very well." He snapped at a servant and barked an order for her items to be prepared on a cart.

"His armor, please, Matilda," Isolde said.

Matilda's horse approached, and she let a package slide from her hands and fall at Gilbert's feet. He gasped in offense and glared up at the maid.

"Mind where your loyalties lie, Brother." Isolde mounted her horse.

Cormac did not immediately follow. He watched Gilbert, his fist clenched as though he wanted to throw a punch. If not more. Finally, he grimaced and climbed onto his steed as well.

Silence descended on them in a thick, suffocating blanket that stifled the air as they waited for Isolde's belongings to be brought to them. Isolde did not waver in her resolve to speak further. She'd said all that was necessary.

However, once the cart joined them, headed by a horse and servant who would no doubt return to Easton upon completion of his task, Isolde could not resist turning to Gilbert one final time.

"I must say, you fought well at the tournament." Isolde smoothed her skirts. "Better than you've ever fought before."

With a smirk, she flicked the reins of her horse and together, along with Pip and Matilda, they turned their horses toward Scotland to their new home and a new life.

EPILOGUE

Five years later

A bove all the sounds on the practice field, it was the clack of wood against wood that caught Cormac's attention. He walked through the rows of men who fought against one another, swords flashing as they thrust and swept out at their opponents.

Attacks from the Ross clan had increased over the years due to the offense of the Sutherland Chieftain stealing away a Ross bride. But the Sutherland clan now consisted of strong people, healthy with an ample supply of food that no one ever ceased being grateful for, and a readiness to defend their land.

Cormac smiled as he came to the outskirts of the mock battle and caught sight of Isolde's auburn hair, swept back in a single braid. Her belly was round and high, filled with their bairn soon to be born.

In her hand, she held a wooden sword that Cormac himself had carved. She lunged forward and gently swung the pretend weapon.

Cormac peered around the men so he could better see the

object of her careful swing; their small daughter, Aila. The lass was only a wee thing, but had the skill and focus for battle like her mum. Alan stood behind both of them with Pip obediently sitting at his side.

Wee Aila blocked her mother's blow, her green eyes focused and assessing as she jabbed her own blunt, wooden sword at Isolde. The sun glinted off her hair, the same auburn as her mother's with silky curls at the ends.

"Very well done," Isolde cheered. "And if I come at you from this side?" She shifted to the left and slowly arced the wooden sword toward their daughter once more.

Aila spun around, the hilt locked in hands still dimpled with youth, her small mouth pinched in concentration as she blocked her mother's gentle swing.

Isolde clapped her hands. "You're such a fine warrior, my love."

The seriousness of Aila's face blossomed into a wide smile. She looked to Pip and slapped her thigh. "Come."

The dog leapt toward her with his tongue lolling happily from the corner of his mouth. He wagged his tail excitedly, flicking eager licks at each in turn and earning laughter from both.

Cormac approached them. "Ye two are the bonniest warriors I've ever seen."

Aila squealed and ran toward him. Cormac caught her mid-run and tossed her high into the air. Her high-pitch shriek cut through the air as he caught her and set her gently to the ground. "I hope ye werena too rough on yer mum."

Aila's eyes went round with sincerity. "Nay, da. I wouldna hurt my brother."

"Your brother?" Isolde put her hand on her stomach. "You're so certain the babe is a boy?"

Aila lifted her little shoulders in a shrug. "Aye. Ye already have a daughter."

Cormac laughed and ruffled Aila's soft hair. She didn't bother to fix it and left her curls rumpled around her face as she grinned up at him. Cormac turned his attention to his beautiful wife and pulled her against him. Her eyes met his, shining with love and her skin glowing with good health. He ran his hand over her belly, and the child within gave a little kick against his palm.

Just as Cormac knew she would be, Isolde had been immediately accepted and loved by the clan who respected her strength as a warrior.

Her dowry had arrived without delay from the Earl of Easton, which marked the last of their communication with her brother. The coin from her dowry had provided enough food to get them through the following winter. The seasons following had been bountiful, and the clan had thrived. The only imperfection in their lives was the wrath of the Rosses, who regularly made their discontent known with raids and attacks.

But it was merely a feud, an offense that would doubtless be forgotten by the next generation. For the time being, Cormac was secure in knowing that his people know how to defend themselves, as did his family.

He hefted Aila to his side with his right arm and tightened his grip with his left arm on Isolde's stretched waist. Both mother and daughter put their heads on his shoulders, filling his senses with the sweetness of sunshine and roses.

His beautiful girls. His beautiful life.

And a joy that could not be dampened by even the bitterest of feuds. Not when Cormac and his family had everything they had ever wanted: food, comfort, protection and love.

"I love you, husband," Isolde said softly near his ear.

He pressed a kiss to her temple. "And I love ye, my lady knight."

Thank you for reading THE HIGHLANDER'S LADY

KNIGHT! I read all of my reviews and love hearing from my readers, so please do leave one.

*** Keep reading for a sneak peek at Chapter 1 of FAYE'S SACRIFICE ***

IF YOU WANT TO FIND OUT MORE ABOUT GRAHAM'S STORY check out the next book in the Midsummer Knights series, THE HIGHLANDER'S DARE by Eliza Knight.

A lady determined to set her own path... A warrior who can't say no to a dare... A love between them would defy all the odds...

Check out all the books in the Midsummer Knights series:
Forbidden Warrior by Kris Kennedy
The Highlander's Lady Knight by Madeline Martin
The Highlander's Dare by Eliza Knight
The Highland Knight's Revenge by Lori Ann Bailey
My Victorious Knight by Laurel O'Donnell
An Outlaw's Honor by Terri Brisbin
Never If Not Now by Madeline Hunter

Sign up for my exclusive newsletter to stay up to date on the latest Borderland Rebels news. Sign up today and get a FREE download THE HIGHLANDER'S CHALLENGE.

www.MadelineMartin/newsletter

FAYE'S SACRIFICE - When the Sutherland-Ross feud continues in generations to come, will a marriage between the Sutherland Chieftain and the granddaughter of the Ross Chieftain heal broken ties? Or will the forced marriage tear them further apart?

Ewan Sutherland, Chieftain of the Sutherland clan, needs an

heir, especially with his uncle intent on claiming the chieftainship.

Faye Fletcher had no plans to marry until she's abducted from her home, dragged to the highlands and forced to wed her grandfather's greatest rival.

When family betrayals and enemy conspiracies threaten to ruin any chance they have of a blissful life together, will Faye let the pain of her past keep her sealed off, or will Ewan's patience and love guide them to happily ever after?

Faye's Sacrifice
Chapter 1 Preview

April 1341
Castleton, Scotland

FAYE FLETCHER HAD AN UNCANNY KNACK FOR GETTING MORE from her coin than others. She scanned an assortment of fabrics, eyeing a blue wool that would suit herself as well as her younger sister, Clara.

"How much?" She settled her fingers on the bolt and raised her eyes to the shopkeeper.

He was younger than she'd expected, and his cheeks colored when their eyes met. "It...it's, uh, three farthings a yard."

She gently caressed the fabric. It was good quality, the color rich as a summer sky. "Three farthings?" she asked, putting an edge of concern in her voice.

The shopkeeper's brow furrowed, mirroring her expression. "Aye."

Faye bit her bottom lip in pensive concentration, and his gaze lowered to her mouth. "I need a dozen yards, but—"

An old man in the alley caught her attention, the same one who had been watching her earlier. He was tall and proud, with a head of red hair threaded with white and wearing a fine black doublet atop leather trews.

His stare bored into her, unabashed and unflinching.

"Mistress?" the shopkeeper asked.

A shudder squeezed up her spine. "I..." She looked to the fabric once more and shook her head. "I've changed my mind."

She swept away from the man's stall without bothering to hear his reply. If he returned to the market another time, she was confident she could smooth over her abrupt departure. Mayhap even use it to elicit sympathy for a further reduction in the cost of the fabric.

Disappointment pricked her. It *had* been fine wool.

She flicked her attention to the alleyway and found the man no longer there. The tension did not ease from her shoulders, however. Instead, wariness tapped at the back of her mind.

She quickened her pace to where she would be meeting with her brother, Drake, on the outskirts of the village. He'd gone to see about getting a cow for them while Faye attended market.

She glanced over her shoulder and found the old man behind her, mere paces away.

"I'd like a word with ye." His voice was gravelly despite his Scottish burr and imbued with the same confidence as his squared shoulders.

She walked more quickly and discreetly slid the dagger from her belt. While she preferred the cut of her own sharp tongue, in a pinch, the blade did quite nicely.

"Mistress Faye Fletcher." Her name on the stranger's lips made her step falter.

She spun around. "I'm not someone ye want to trifle with."

He lifted his brows with apparent amusement and swept his gaze over her. "Ye've grown into a bonny lass."

"And ye're a leering old goat."

He tsked. "Is that any way to speak to yer grandda?"

The apprehension in Faye's gut drew into a hard knot. She

met his green eyes, a shade disconcertingly similar to her mum's. Prickles ran over her flesh.

She'd heard enough about him to be wary. He was Chieftain of the Ross clan, a man with power and greed running in his cold veins. He was so cruel and self-serving that Mum had risked her family starving rather than take her children to live near Balnagown Castle in the highlands.

Faye glared at him. "My grandda is a dishonorable cur who rules with fear and manipulation. If ye are indeed who ye claim to be, I want nothing to do with ye."

The mirth fled his expression, and his face went red under his rust-colored beard. "Impudent chit." He narrowed his eyes at her. "It doesna matter what ye want. I've come to fetch ye to deliver ye to yer betrothed."

She tightened her grip on her dagger. Betrothed? What was he on about?

She scoffed derisively to cover her unease. "Ye're mad and I dinna have time for this."

She turned away and strode swiftly toward the large tree where she'd planned to meet Drake, hoping to God he was already waiting. Her grandda's strong, wiry grasp caught her arm and spun her back toward him.

This was exactly why she carried a blade. She rolled her arm over his and gripped his thick wrist, twisting it sharply. He grunted in pain, but she didn't stop there.

Quick as a blink, she put the point of her dagger to his withered throat. "Leave me be and dinna bother coming to find my family, or I willna stop my blade next time, aye?"

He grimaced, his teeth yellow beneath his thin lips. "Let go of me, ye impertinent chit."

She shoved him from her, then backed away.

"Ye willna go unpunished for that." He glowered at her, then slipped between two homes, disappearing.

Faye slowly exhaled, and a tremble softened her limbs. Was he the man he said he was? Her grandda? And what was his claim of her being betrothed?

She kept the dagger clutched in her grasp as she made her way to the large tree. Drake was already waiting for her with a velvety brown cow whose soft eyes were large and framed with long lashes.

Drake frowned as she approached. "What is it, Faye?"

There was a single moment that passed where she considered telling him what had happened. But only one before she resolved to keep news of their grandfather's presence in the village to herself.

Drake was the eldest of the four of them and had been visiting the last sennight. The following morning, he was due to return to the English side of the border to resume his duty as Captain of the Guard at Werrick Castle.

His job was one of great importance and brought him an abundance of pride. It was not the knighthood he'd hoped to obtain as their father had, but it was an honorable position in a notable household. One that afforded them all a much better life than the one they'd had before.

No longer were they forced to wear threadbare clothes that kept them chilled in the winter. Nor go without food so long that their bellies snarled with hunger.

She was grateful for what he did for them, but did not care for him being gone so long or being so far away-especially at a place where his heart had been broken by one of the earl's daughters. Her handsome brother should have already have a wife and children, and she suspected his lack of procuring one had a good deal to do with Lady Anice.

If Drake knew their grandfather was nearby, and that Faye had been approached, he would undoubtedly delay his return to Werrick Castle. She wouldn't have Drake risk his job on her account. Not when they were finally doing so well, in a stone manor outside the village with several livestock and enough food and clothing to be comfortable.

"'Tis only that I'm sad ye'll be leaving us on the morrow." Faye gave her brother a perfect smile. A lifetime of practice had rendered the expression convincing.

Drake's worry lightened into an endearing expression, and he ruffled her hair. "I'll be back before ye start to miss me."

She smoothed her fingers over her tresses to ensure his affection hadn't left her mussed. "But I already miss ye, and ye've not even left yet."

He chuckled. "Ach, my honey-tongued sister. One day ye're going to get yerself in trouble with such pretty words."

"I'm sure I'll find a way out of it." She grinned.

Together, they wandered down the trail leading to the stone manor Drake had constructed for them two years prior. It had taken several years to save enough, but the home provided them with protection for themselves, as well as their livestock.

Faye's meeting with the old man churned in her thoughts, though she'd tried to set it aside. Later, she would gently prod her mother for information on the alleged betrothal. If there were any truth to the Ross Chieftain's words, Faye would be able to ease it from her mother without suspicion.

Regarding the chieftain himself, he was nothing Faye couldn't handle. After all, how much of a threat could one old man be?

Sutherland, Scotland

EWAN SUTHERLAND, CHIEFTAIN OF THE SUTHERLAND CLAN, was getting married. Again.

Or at least, he would be promised to the chieftain's daughter of the Gordon clan once he stroked his signature over the lengthy agreement set before him. The quill remained perched in his fingertips, the point not quite settled upon the page. A drop of ink slid from the sharpened tip and beaded on the parchment before absorbing into a blotch of black.

"Ye dinna want to marry the lass?" Monroe asked from his seat opposite Ewan's desk.

Ewan lifted his head to regard his advisor as he considered the question.

Mistress Blair Gordon was fine enough. Ewan had met her several times at a feast held by the Gordon clan. She'd been a talkative young woman whose face dipped demurely to the ground any time her father was nearby.

There had been a girlish excitement about her, not at all like the formal stiffness of Lara. The thought of his first wife brought an uncomfortable tightness to his chest.

Why then was he so opposed to signing the damn betrothal contract?

Ewan set the quill aside.

"Ach, that's what I thought." Monroe's dark brows twitched. "There may be another option."

"I canna remain unwed," Ewan grumbled bitterly.

He didn't want a wife. But he needed an heir. And alas, one could not come without the other. Or at least, not a *legitimate* heir. And he wouldn't complicate a lad's life with having him be born a bastard.

"I dinna mean ye should remain unwed." Monroe smoothed a hand over the heavy wooden chair arm and scanned the capacious solar as though seeking to ensure their privacy, despite their being alone. "Though yer uncle remains curiously quiet over the matter."

"Curious," Ewan repeated bitterly. "I dinna expect him to support a union where an heir might prevent him from inheriting the title of chieftain should I die. We all know he's been eyeing it since my da passed."

Ewan rubbed at a knot of tension at the back of his neck. Having his uncle in his close council allowed Ewan to maintain a watchful eye on him, but it didn't mean the task was easy or pleasant.

Ewan's cousin, Moiré, kept abreast of her father's activities to ensure they were not nefarious. She had come to be something like a sister to him. Without any sisters of his own and with his elder brother having passed years ago, Ewan found himself often seeking her counsel and relying upon her for duties in the castle after Lara's death.

"Ye received a missive from the Chieftain of the Ross clan." Monroe withdrew a folded bit of parchment from the pocket of his doublet. "It arrived by messenger moments ago. The lad informed me it had something to do with yer betrothal."

"My betrothal?" Ewan took the letter, cracked the thick seal depicting a hand holding a laurel wreath and unfolded it to read the contents within.

Once done, he lowered the parchment to the top of his desk in wonder. "Faye Fletcher."

"I'd nearly forgotten about her," Monroe confessed.

"As had I." Ewan pushed up from his hard, wooden seat and approached the fireplace where the flames licked over dry tinder. "But it was never signed by her mother. 'Tis no' binding."

He hadn't seen Faye since they were children—when she'd left after a visit from England and had never returned. It was why she'd slipped from his thoughts for so long.

Faye Fletcher had been a quiet, sweet girl who had always seemed so delicate with her slim frame and pale blonde hair and blue eyes. She'd be a biddable lass; that's what his da had said of her. Granddaughter to the Ross Chieftain, she and Ewan would bring peace to their clans. Their union was made to melt the hatred of the last two centuries and unite the clans as one.

Ewan recalled his hope at such an idea. But he was no longer a lad swayed by fanciful notions. He was a man who led other men. His decisions dictated who lived and who died.

"What does her dowry offer?" Monroe asked.

Ewan folded his arms over his chest. "A considerable amount of coin, more so than what the Gordon lass brings, as well as lands to the west of us and...peace." He sniffed at the ridiculousness of the latter.

Unfortunately, the offer was a tempting one. The lands to the west were rich and ideal for raising sheep. With the cost of wool rising, it would be an ideal opportunity to amass wealth. As of late, the constant battles between clans had been expensive.

A marriage to Mistress Faye Fletcher would resolve both issues, as well as hopefully provide him with an heir.

Monroe turned in his chair to face Ewan so that his dark, smooth hair gleamed in the firelight. "How much land does the Ross lass bring?"

"A considerable amount." Ewan returned to his desk and regarded the letter once more. "More than they'll get from Berwick. I dinna know why they've wanted that land for so long." Berwick was over a fortnight's journey away and overrun with reivers and thieves. The Sutherland clan hadn't bothered to maintain any sense of order there. Such a feat was near impossible.

"Ross insists that I consider the betrothal and meet with him next month to discuss its renewal." Sutherland glanced at the agreement beside the letter, the one that would seal him to Mistress Blair Gordon.

The girl Faye had been rose in his thoughts. What kind of a woman would she be now? Had her skinny body blossomed out to be more robust? Had her white-blonde hair stayed fair or turned the color of wheat?

"What will ye do?" Monroe asked.

Ewan's chest constricted at the thought of marrying again. Lara had been a good wife to him. She had not bickered or complained, nor had she desperately clung to him as some men's wives did. She had performed her duties at the castle promptly and in good order. Aye, she had not given him a bairn in their three years together, but she had tried.

It had been almost two years since her death and Ewan was not getting any younger. He required a wife and a son and had two contracts lying at his fingertips. He heaved a sigh that sent the parchments shifting over the desk.

"Aye," he said at last, his mind finally made up. "I'll meet with Ross to discuss the possibility of marriage to Mistress Faye Fletcher."

AUTHOR'S NOTE

Writing about the 12th century was an unfamiliar era for me as I generally write from the 14th century on. It doesn't seem like 200 years could really make that big of a difference, but it certainly did! As with all my books, I dug into the research and found some interesting facts I, of course, must share!

First of all, believe me when I say that the stirrups and high-backed seat of a saddle were huge inventions of this time. Before these items came about, riders couldn't safely go to battle on horseback as a single blow (delivered or received) would knock them easily from their horse. The stirrups and high-backed saddle allowed a warrior to brace themselves on their steeds and charge into battle without the danger of being unseated. Before those items came about, knights would ride to the location of battle, dismount and tether their horses, then fight on foot. Sure brings a different image to a knight when he's not on his horse in combat, doesn't it?

Jousting tournaments were pretty dangerous, but early medieval ones were especially so. We touch on some items in our stories in this series, like how death is possible regardless of how safe things are intended to be. But death was very possible, not just by the nobles who were engaged in the tournament, but for the peasants as well.

It wasn't uncommon for the lines of the melee to flex out and ultimately include villager's homes. During this time, knights were determined to capture one another at any cost. They were also willing to avoid capture at any cost. This meant villager's homes became battle grounds. Yeah, it's as bad as it sounds Sometimes peasants were accidental casualties of these mock battles and other times their homes could be burned down and they would be left with nothing. Of course, we refrained from mentioning this in our books as all of our knights were respectful of the peasants and all around good people. Bravo to our heroes and heroines!

But jousting had its dangers as well. Weapons were not blunted in the time period we wrote in (we used creative liberty to blunt them for our stories), which meant a higher likelihood of death or critical maiming in combat. Additionally, there was not a 'tilt' which is the barrier running between the jousters to separate them. Without it, jousters would sometimes collide head on – with fatal results.

Before this project, I never appreciated the dangers truly faced by these men who jousted and participated in tournaments. I hope you've enjoyed reading about it as I did truly had a wonderful time unearthing it all and hope you are enjoying this series as well! Thank you SO much for reading!

ACKNOWLEDGMENTS

THANK YOU TO my amazing beta readers who helped make this story so much more with their wonderful suggestions: Tracy Emro and Lorrie Cline. You ladies are so amazing and make my books just shine!

Thank you to my amazing editor, Erica Monroe with Quillfire Author Services. You make my books so much better and keep me laughing in the process.

Thank you to Janet Kazmirski for the final read-through you always do for me and for catching all the little last minute tweaks.

Thank you to John and my wonderful minions for all the support they give me.

And a huge thank you so much to my readers for always being so fantastically supportive and eager for my next book.

ABOUT THE AUTHOR

Madeline Martin is a USA TODAY Bestselling author of Scottish set historical romance novels filled with twists and turns, adventure, steamy romance, empowered heroines and the men who are strong enough to love them.

She lives a glitter-filled life in Jacksonville, Florida with her two daughters (known collectively as the minions) and a man so wonderful he's been dubbed Mr. Awesome. She loves Disney, Nutella, cat videos and goats dressed up in pajamas. She also loves to travel and attributes her love of history to having spent most of her childhood as an Army brat in Germany.

Find out more about Madeline at her website:

http://www.madelinemartin.com

 facebook.com/MadelineMartinAuthor

 twitter.com/MadelineMMartin

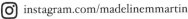 instagram.com/madelinemmartin

 bookbub.com/profile/madeline-martin

.

Manufactured by Amazon.ca
Bolton, ON

13742602R00106